Wisely Stupid

About the Author

Zeeshan Najafi hails from Bangalore. Currently he is working in Amazon.com. He is a Business Management graduate and pursuing his Master's degree in Philosophy. He is fond of Sufi literature and enjoys reading books on mysticism, philosophy and poetry.

Najafi is a passionate reader and likes travelling, writing poetry and philosophical essays. He collects books and has his personal library.

To know more about him, please log on to *www.zeeshannajafi.com* or you can reach him at *zeeshannajafi@gmail.com, www.facebook.com/mmzeeshan.*

Wisely Stupid

A Story of 'What Matters'

Zeeshan Najafi

GENERAL PRESS

Published by
GENERAL PRESS
4228/1, Ansari Road, Daryaganj
New Delhi – 110002
Ph. : 011 – 23282971, 45795759
e-mail : generalpressindia@gmail.com

www.generalpress.in

First Edition : February 2013

ISBN : 9789380914398

Published by Azeem Ahmad Khan for General Press

Dedication

All praise to God, who helps me in each endeavour. I dedicate this work to all the wise men for inspiring me with their infinite wisdom and my parents for their love, kindness and support.

Acknowledgements

I appreciate all the events and catastrophes which led to the completion of this book. I thank my dear ones for their support and trust in me, especially Amish for being a part of my life. I also thank the one who asked me to write this book.

Preface

Whom alas shall I complain, when sin wanders in every soul and imperfection exists in every pleasure?

Are we the product of an accident, who accidentally happened to be on this earth at this point of time without a purpose? Do we have a free will or are we just living according to someone's plan?

What is this Longing and Loneliness which keeps bothering us all the time? Does it have an end?

How often do we get a chance to take a step back and ponder over our lives?

Here is a story which will help you to solve the complicated riddles of your life.

1
Combat with the Self

Indeed we gain new perspectives concerning every kind of reality sooner or later in our lives. Not everyone wants to be awakened from daydreaming in an ordinary life.

It all started when I entered into a retrospective mode in life. I think it's worth pondering over things I never thought existed in this apparently mundane life. The restlessness caused is nerve breaking as random thoughts keep multiplying incessantly in my mind. I am stuck in a maze which has no exit and the emotional crisis makes me despondent.

Is there something more profound besides the seeming incompleteness of life? I ask myself this question, finding it very difficult to garner any response. I experience panic attacks every day, feeling like I am dying and being resurrected all at once. This is what it feels like when everything you anticipate just ceases to exist in an instant and you are asked to start a new life altogether without a clue.

I am caught in a limbo, transfixed, uncertain of my thought process. I try to block my negative thoughts but they keep haunting me every passing second. I need to vent my frustration, I need someone to speak my heart out to, but I find none around me. All my desperation is of no avail because people around me are busy simplifying their own complex life. No one has time enough to counsel my rather disturbed thoughts.

Every time I make an attempt to distract myself something more excruciating possibly finds me, fuelling my already worse condition, magnifying my ambiguity, like a snowball growing in size as it rolls down the steep hill. I have had enough. All I want now is to free myself of the kind of life I am living. I want to live a different, less pretentious and more real life, like a free man who is not bound by clocks or calendars. I want to perceive the world with a renewed and positive outlook, which will be easily receptive to my susceptible mind.

It's just not me; people are worse than dogs. We always end up chasing the stone, instead of chasing the one who throws it at us. I want to access the root of my troubles.

I want to unburden myself off with the kind of life I am living. I feel like I have been domesticated and I have camouflaged my appearance in an abstract personality to look normal, and when I try to think about the future, all I see is the catastrophe waiting to embrace me with arms wide open. The irony is there is no escape from it; even if there is an escape, who could possibly know?

There are many unanswered questions that keep pestering my mind, giving me a nervous breakdown. I was caught and duped in this unreality all this while and now that I want to exit, I see no way out. Did I have a perfect life? Was I living in an imperfect world? Of course, they are both very different questions.

Whatever happened with me today has had a profound reason, and it was not just an accident. They say, "Any day above the ground is a blessing." I think this statement has to be rephrased as "any unblessed day on the ground is not a day." How long should I pretend to be happy? How long should I await for the silver lining to emerge out of the dense clouds?

I couldn't stay obtuse anymore. I took an extreme step today and I did not succeed and after that I encountered something that not only changed my mental situation, but also alleviated me. It is 2 a.m. in the morning and I am sitting in my room, staring at the wall and hoping for a solution, a way out of the mess. I experienced something strange today which I believe no other soul has. But before that, let me tell you how that fateful day unfolded.

It was Monday, first day of the week in the calendar, I woke up at 6 a.m. in the morning with a similar obnoxious feelings. It has been a week since I last went to work and I had this gut feeling that my job would be at stake if I don't go to the office today. So I dared and decided to take on things as they come my way. I popped one tranquilliser and left my home at 8 a.m. My office is an hour's drive from where I live. I started my car and for a change, took a new route to work. My choice led me to the same old road I use to take to college years ago. There was a coffee shop around the corner where I used to hang around during my college days, to get the feel of my good old college days. I pulled over to have a cup of coffee there.

On entering the cafe, my heartbeat rose and it thumped against my ribcage. This was not new for me. I was not scared of it any more. It was just another panic attack. I sat quietly for ten minutes until I felt better. The truth is I haven't understood yet as to why this happens to me. I had another mood swing and I decided not to go to work today and thought of taking a resolute decision about my life. I started pondering over the events that occurred in my life. I did a lot of introspection on what I was doing, and what I did in my past and on things that I intend to do in future. In all the flashbacks and flash-forwards, I couldn't see any positive outcome. When you take a step back and think on these aspects, it's hard to continue a normal life, and it gets worse when you are forced to live one.

Everything has a breaking point; even the sun breaks down by the end of the day. They say only cowards commit suicide. I am not a coward; I just can't take it any more. It is far better to vanish before you are banished. I have insisted enough that I live by materialism and it's high time I end this miserable life. I am now convinced that this isn't the place for me. Who knows? There could be a better world after death. Honestly, I don't have anyone who'll truly miss me when I am gone. My parents may mourn over my death for a couple of months and they will move on; my friends will leave obituary messages on my facebook page for a while, but they too will move on, like everyone else. Oh! I forgot, my so-called girlfriend and the love of my life who left me, may say, "I didn't ask him to die; he was a psycho from the beginning."

A suicide note seemed perfect. But I censured the proposition because I had no idea to whom should I address it to. And out of all the suicidal ideas that occupied my mind, I thought hanging by a noose would be most convenient. I couldn't afford to buy a gun nor could I muster enough courage to jump off a building. I finished the last coffee of my life and switched on my laptop to Google for effective hanging techniques; while I was browsing I remembered movies where they used perfect hanging ropes to choke someone to death. After a few seconds, I found out the way to tie a knot; it was called the *hangman's knot*. Now, all I needed was a rope which could bear my weight and squeeze out my life. I went to a nearby supermarket to buy the rope.

I went inside and asked the salesman behind the counter, "Do you keep ropes?"

"What for?" asked the salesman.

Obviously, I wouldn't tell him why. I asked him to show me a long rope. He pointed out to the corner and said, "You can check there, sir."

I walked to where he pointed. They had all hardware and plumbing items stacked, and along with those were the ropes – of all kinds. I couldn't find the thick white rope like I imagined. But I found a bundle of colourful fibre ropes which could do the job. I bought two bundles. At the back of my mind I wondered about my bad luck, what if something went wrong and I survived? I got back in the car and did some more research on the survival consequences of unsuccessful suicide. I found some terrible things that could happen to me if I survived.

The process was this; when I hang myself, my neck will break immediately due to the pressure, and oxygen supply to the brain will stop, and it may take 15 to 20 minutes to die. If something goes wrong with the knot, and if my hanging is not proper, I may just hang and struggle until someone finds out, and it may cause serious brain injury that can paralyse my whole body. No way can I bear something like that. I mean, I can't be paralysed for the rest of my life and become a burden for someone else. Shit, I was so happy to end this miserable life but now I am scared, what if something goes wrong. I wish Bangalore had a beach; I would have thrown myself into the sea. I wish these heavy overhead electric cables would fall on me and solve my problem.

I failed even before I made an attempt. I dumped myself in the car with the pathetic feeling of not being able to die. I smoked around 10 cigarettes and kept thinking what to do next. Suddenly it came to my mind what the priest had told me once. He had said: "When you are too depressed or when you are too happy, go visit a graveyard. It will bring you back to your normal sense."

It was around 1 p.m. in the afternoon. I decided to go and spend some time in the graveyard. There was a cemetery next to the school where I studied, and that was the only peaceful place I could think of going. I immediately drove to that place and reached there within 30 minutes.

The cemetery was a quasi antiquity, spread over a vast area. I parked my car and walked inside; my head was feeling heavy because I was hungry but I was in no mood to have anything. Every bench I tried to sit on was either broken or dirty. There was a banyan tree in the middle of the graveyard, under which I found a bench which was half covered with dry leaves. I cleaned it and comfortably seated myself. Initially I just looked at tombstones and imagined how my tombstone would look. We engage ourselves in so many activities but we never think about designing our tombstone.

I could still hear the cacophony of traffic from outside. A cool breeze was flowing inside the cemetery, which eased my nerves and the rustling leaves of the banyan tree made me appreciate the peacefulness of the place. I sat quietly on the bench for almost an hour and I didn't feel restless at all; may be I was able to relate myself with the dead in the graves. After all, it's going to be the final resting place, where we have to settle down even if we don't like it. I found some broken sticks; I picked one and started drawing something on the ground. Of course, an idle man can do anything to keep himself busy. I spent around two to three hours in the graveyard, doing aimless things and my purpose of being there was served. I decided to visit the graveyard once a week regularly. It was around 4 p.m., when I decided to leave the place. While I was going out, a green van entered the graveyard and the man who was sealed next to the driver waved his hand. I wasn't sure if that was for me or for someone else. Anyway, I left the place.

2
Highly Unlikely

There was a traffic signal right next to the graveyard's compound, where lights had turned red just before I could take a right turn. I made the car's engine dead and took a sigh of relief. While I was lost in my thoughts, a man approached my car from behind and knocked at the window. As I rolled it down, he blurted panting, "*Bhaisahab!* I need your help, Can you help me?"

I turned around; it was the same guy from the green van who had waved at me. His face was contoured with tension.

I agreed to help him.

"Can you please come with me to the cemetery?" he pleaded.

I was kind of confused looking at him; he mumbled something again, but I was unable to follow him. He was excessively sweating while trying to catch his breath.

"Fine, let's go."

I parked my car across the street and started walking towards the cemetery with him. While I was walking, I asked him again, "What has happened? Is something wrong?"

He didn't answer; I could only hear his irregular sobs.

I entered the cemetery and saw two men standing next to the van; one of them was the driver of the van. I again queried, but this time from the driver, "What's wrong?"

He shrugged without saying anything and looked at the other guy. The guy I came with, opened the back door of the van and to my horror, there was a dead body inside, neatly wrapped in a spotless shroud.

It was a rare sight for me, it made me irksome and I asked the guy again, but this time rudely, "Excuse me! What's the matter? Whose body is this?"

The other guy walked up to me straight and in a low voice said, "My name is Sam and this is my friend Kabir and the deceased person who has repelled you so much is Kabir's mother."

Suddenly, Kabir spoke out in grief, "Sir, could you please help us with the burial."

I was amazed and asked, "Don't you have any relatives or friends to help you with the burial? Are you new in Bangalore? How did she die?"

My constant firing of questions was odd at that moment, but I could not desist at the end of this flurry. He only answered, "Right now, I don't have anyone. Please help me if you can. I thought the grave-diggers would already be here but I don't see them around. I think they left before we reached. If you are uncomfortable, I can understand. I'll wait for some more time until I get somebody."

He still had tears in his eyes while he faked a smile to make the situation appear normal to me.

I don't think he was sarcastic; he was just too helpless at that moment. I said "NO! Just tell me what I need to do." He thanked me and we started the proceedings.

The driver asked me if I could sit in the front seat of the van as they had to go a little further to a corner where the grave had been dug. He took a left turn and went a little further. Sam asked the driver to park the van next to the corner wall. The van stopped. Kabir and Sam got down from the back seat and lifted the casket and kept it on the mud hill next to the grave. The driver locked all the doors of the van and came to the site.

I stood nervously next to the van, biting my nails and wondered, "What's happening here?"

Kabir waved his hand like he did earlier. Now I knew he was calling me and I went straight to him.

"Excuse me! I didn't get your name."

"I am Jako, I mean Jackson," I replied.

"Sam and I are going to get down the grave; and all we want you guys to do is move the casket and deliver it to us."

It didn't sound complicated. I said, "Fine, I can do that."

Kabir and Sam jumped into the grave. Kabir was still wiping his tears, standing inside and Sam tried to console him, saying, "I know this is a tough time for you, but you have to be strong here."

Is this the way somebody consoles you, when you are about to bury your mother? I was quietly observing Kabir and Sam. Sam held Kabir's shivering hand and said, "Bro, I am with you, don't worry."

He looked up and asked the driver to hold one side of the casket and asked me to hold it from the other side; we moved the casket towards the grave. There were two knots to that wrapped cloth, one over the head and another at the feet. Sameer asked us to hold the knots, lift the body and pass it to them.

The moment I heard it, I cried, "I am sorry. I can't do this. I have never touched a dead body before."

Sam came out and said, "Jackson, you just have to hold the knot and lift it."

"I am sorry, Sam, I have never done this before," I said.

"Me too…I am just trying to help," Sam said.

Finally, I agreed, and Sam got down again. I held the knot at the feet's end and the driver held it from the other side. The body was heavy to lift and I had to pass it to Kabir. Kabir raised his hands and looked at me, waiting for the body to be delivered. My hands started shivering and I lost control over my grip. It slipped from my hands and the body fell down. Sameer shouted, "Jackson! Slowly man, what are you doing?"

"I told you, I haven't done this before. I am sorry, I can't do this," I said.

Sam came up and said, "Jackson, I know it's difficult. Do one thing, I'll move the body from top. The driver is old and he can't lift it."

"So what do you want me to do?" I asked.

"You get down and help Kabir. All you have to do is, hold the knot tightly and Kabir will do the rest."

"What? You want me to get inside the grave? Sorry man, there's no way I am going down into that creepy grave."

"Even I am embarrassed by asking you to do this bro. It's getting dark, it will take a few minutes. Please help," Sam said.

I had no choice but to agree. I said, "Okay, let's do it."

Sam asked me to take off my shoes; maybe it was the part of the custom. I didn't ask anything more and got into the grave. The surface was wet and those mud walls around drove me crazy. My heartbeat sank and rose in crescendo. When I looked up from down under, it was the scariest sight I had ever witnessed in my whole life. Sam and the driver were looking down from top; I couldn't even blink my eyes. I thought I was getting buried there. My whole body went numb and I was dead with fear. Sam called out my name, "Jackson! Are you ready?"

I was too blank to reply anything. I looked at Kabir and said, "Yes."

They both lifted the dead body and gave it to us. I held the knot which was tied on the head and Kabir was on the other side. Sam asked me to place the body slowly on the ground. I couldn't move an inch. I just held the knot tightly. Kabir placed the body from his side and Sam shouted again, "Just place it." I was in a shock and I couldn't keep the grip tight anymore and dropped it abruptly. As soon as the body hit the ground, the knot opened and the old lady's face came out of the shroud. I bent down to tie the knot again. When I got closer, a reeking smell came out of her mouth; which was indescribable; it was beyond words. My senses froze and I found it difficult to inhale the air. I was frightened to death and shrieked, "Oh God, What's this?"

"Jackson, give me your hand." Sam shouted from top. He grabbed my hand and pulled me out.

"What did you do, man?" he asked.

I couldn't utter a word. And how could I? I didn't even look back at the grave and moved away from that place.

Sam might have jumped inside and tied that loosened knot and performed the other rituals. But, for me, I had done enough. I was unable to take anything happening around me anymore. I mean, what worse could happen to someone like me? It was a completely soul-shaking experience. Though I was transfixed at a spot, I anyhow managed to walk away from there. I walked to the other corner and sat down on a bench. My jaw joints were jammed and my head was spinning like a top. After some time, all three of them took their shovels and covered the grave. Kabir walked up to me and said, "Thanks bro, thanks for everything."

I had no words to tell him anything or to console him. All I could say was, "It's fine and you take care." He shook my hand and rode away in the van.

After they left the place, I sat on that bench telling myself, 'That's it, you'll be brought to an abandoned place when you are helpless from every part of your body. After that you will be covered by a heap of earth and then they'll start their vehicles and go away, leaving you behind forever.'

Had the old lady been given a chance, what would have she said? How does one feels when it's left behind all alone in the hole? I felt so lonely and become crazy after Deepa had left me. Not only she, everyone who claims to love me – my parents and friends, all are going to do the same thing. No one is going to accompany me in that dark grave because no one loves and cares for me that much. Never have I heard anybody sleeping with their loved ones in the grave. Once they cover you with loads of mud, there's no way out. All my life, I thought that people will join me on two occasions – on my wedding and on my funeral. Now I am unsure about the second occasion.

For some reason, I was feeling very guilty. There was something I was regretting. The moment I saw the lady's face, I was moved towards something – maybe towards myself. It's not necessary that your eyes should be wide open and you need to have an expression on your face to convey the message. I think that dead lady taught me something. I sat there for some more time, looking at the graves and wondered, *what was happening six feet under? Isn't it suffocating?* I saw around fifty tombstones there, but there was no consistency in age group. There were kids, young and middle-aged men and the old ones. I always thought I was going to die, when I would turn too old and feeble.

Each one in these graves has gone through the same process. It's just that I wasn't aware of it. All my future plans, so-called love, career plans, goals, family, friends, money…everything appeared hazy, unclear and obscure. I had just one question, *who will accompany me here?* Oh God! How well I am being duped. All I had, all I have and all that I may have would end here? I don't even know what matters and what doesn't at this moment. Was I chasing a ghost all my life? Why didn't I see all this before? Was I mistaken all this time?

I thought, 'No, I did what I had to do, or more precisely I did what was expected out of me. I knew about death, but didn't know what happens after that and how will I get treated? This is so apparent now. Even if I start introspecting on what's wrong, where do I begin? Should I blame someone now?'

Whoever, I think of blaming, in the end it comes and stops at me. I felt like I had wasted my entire life right from the beginning. But on the other side, I was glad to experience what I did today. I was oblivious about my state and I wanted to think straight and figure out things.

When I walked into this cemetery, I had no clue what was in store for me. I am sure everything happens for a reason. I left the place and took the same left turn and again the traffic light turned red on me. I stopped and looked back; I was just checking if someone was looking for burial help. This time there was no one but the empty street. Light turned green; I crossed the cemetery's compound and hit the road which was busy as usual. People were driving their vehicles and continuously honking. All were rushing towards something which they think is going to last forever. I managed to drive away from the busy road and made my way home.

3

Black Clouds with Silver Linings

It was around 7 p.m., my Dad was back from work. He is a police officer and had always considered work his worship. He has 11 months to go for his retirement and he's severely depressed about it. He thinks it's the end of his world. Yes, it's tough for someone who has spent 30 years doing the same job. He's worried about not being a cop anymore. After this, who's going to salute him anymore? I think this is what he's going to miss the most – the salutes. He was in no mood to listen to my story and even if he was, I was sure that he would yell at me, after listening to it. He doesn't even know that I have stopped going to work since the past one week. I'll have a list of questions to answer if I want to talk to him about the incident. But beyond all that I was glad to see him; honestly I was happy to see him alive. My Mom is in USA since one month with my sister who's settled in Seattle.

I wanted to make sure that my Mom was keeping good health in an entirely new place. So I called and spoke to her for a few minutes. She asked me if I wanted to speak to my sister, but I denied. There's no point talking to someone who cannot imagine what I had gone through. As far as my relationship with my elder sister is concerned, I was never able to connect with her from childhood. And she proved it when she became an engineer. I am not against engineers, but I am against all those who spend their lives studying mathematics. To be frank, I have a tendency to dislike all those who like mathematics. I was not good at mathematics back in my school days and that was the only subject in which I scored less. I hated numbers. I tried figuring out why I hated mathematics so much. I got my answer when I was in graduation when one of my friends asked me to read a book which he thought was really inspiring. It was the *The Autobiography of Malcolm X.* It was indeed an inspiring book because even Malcolm X hated mathematics and he answered my question which had haunted me since my school days – why is that I don't like mathematics? In his autobiography, Malcolm X said, he hates mathematics because "there's no room for argument in that." That was the exact answer which I was looking to justify my hatred. It is so obvious because you can't think of anything when 2+2 is 4. There is no out-of-the-box thinking required when you have defined formulas. It was not just my sister; I couldn't really connect with anyone who was an expert in mathematics.

This was one of the reasons I loved Deepa, my ex-girlfriend. She had expressed her hatred towards mathematics several times. But then, what was the use of it? She left me a couple of weeks back as she found a big shot engineer. I thought she hated engineers but time reveals the truth after all. Deepa was the only person I had imagined to spend my entire life with. Every night before I went to sleep, I used to listen to her sweet voice. I use to speak to her every morning after I woke up. Eventually I started loving her more than I was supposed to. I was crazy enough to do anything for her; I thought she really meant it, when she used to utter those three beautiful words, 'I love you'. Everything suddenly stopped when she suddenly dumped me for silly reasons. I still can't figure out the real reason. I think she wanted to settle down with someone who was career oriented, money minded an ideal family man and less psyched person, unlike me. She was no different than other girls; it was my mistake that I thought she was different and special. But still I wish she was here now so that I could tell her everything that had happened to me today. I thought about it for a while and decided to give her a call. I knew she wouldn't answer the call from my number. I went out and called from a phone booth, and as I had expected, she answered it.

"Hi, what's up?" Jako here.

"What do you want from me Jackson?"

"I just want to talk to you."

"I am really busy now and I think it's all over now. You should stop calling me."

"I really need to talk to you about something."

"Jako, I told you it's not going to work out. I really like you, but it's not going to work out anymore. We belong to different worlds; nothing is similar in our lives, our family, religion, culture, ideas, aspirations, destination, nothing is similar. They exist is contradiction, in opposition. Jako there is no match possible in our case."

"It's not about that Deepa. Please listen to me. I really need you now."

The moment I said that, she disconnected the call. I tried calling her for next 10 minutes, but all in vain. After some time she sent me a message – *'You have already made my life miserable; don't make it worse.'*

I replied to her – *'I won't; please talk to me once.'* I knew she wouldn't reply and that was her last message to me.

When people don't explain themselves, they leave the door open for assumptions. I stopped being emotional for a moment and looked back. This is not the first time this happened. There were times when I used to break down, crying before her and she used to walk out on me saying, "I can't take your drama anymore."

And later she would bring up our religious differences to fight. I mean, we could have fought over other things; why religion? After all, both of us were not religious. The bottom line was she found for herself a Mr. Perfect in all aspects. And right now, there's no point talking sense into her as her mind was influenced by all the fake pomposity. I was not committed to her; I think I was dedicated to her. And now I am paying the price for it. May be it's my anger which is making me blabber all this now, but I strongly feel that she was more than what I needed and less than what I deserved.

I am an atheist, because I just can't follow something because my parents do so or expect me to do. How can I consider them to be right with religion when I consider them to be wrong at everything else?

Anyway, I came inside and locked myself in my room; I didn't feel like eating anything. I crashed on to my bed and started staring at the empty wall and trying to fish out the concealed answer of my strange thoughts from it.

Where did this all begin? Who am I and what did I do all this time? This was the first time I mustered the courage to step back and give a second thought.

I was born as a premature baby at seven months and my twin brother died 10 minutes after birth. Only God knows what made him give up and what made me stay. I am 24 now and my Dad says that 'I look like his grandfather'. How convenient – my great grandfather died ages before there was any photography. I completed my formal education without any big obstacle. My Dad wanted me to become a police officer. He kept pestering me to prepare for civil services after my graduation. It wasn't a big deal for me to take the IPS exam, but I chose to pursue MBA as I was going through other mental problems which would make it difficult for me to prepare for the exam which was very demanding because I started getting panic attacks when I was 20.

It was Christmas. I was about to meet my old friends and cousins and I was happy about it. I came back home and had a fine dinner with my family and went to bed. It was around 2 when I got up with a jolt of sudden pain in my chest. My heart was knocking at the ribcage and I was perspiring terribly. I drank water and sat straight for a while. I felt as if my heart would burst out any moment. I tried to convince myself that nothing was wrong and the reason of my ill-health was a hectic day, but it was of no help. I felt horrible each passing moment. It was then I realised that something was wrong with me. One of my cousins was at home that night.

I woke him up and said, "Dude, will you come with me to the hospital? I am having chest pain."

"It may be because you smoked too many cigarettes today," he said.

I knew it was not because of smoking; it was something else. I forced him to take me to the hospital. I was attended by the emergency doctor who asked me if this had happened before. I informed him that this was the first time I was going through this. He took my ECG and the results were normal. He then gave me a sleeping pill as he thought it'll help me if I sleep for some time. That was the first time I took a sleeping pill. I came back and didn't tell anybody at home what had happened at night. Everything was normal after I woke up and I felt better after the long sleep. After a couple of days, I felt the same pain erupting during daytime when I was in college.

It felt as if I was going to die in a few minutes. I had an immense pain in my chest which was unbearable. It lasted for a few minutes and after that, I was absolutely normal. I had no idea what was happening. I again didn't inform anyone about this.

This thing continued for almost two years. I used to visit the hospital regularly when it got worse. I tried to handle it myself whenever I could. I realised that the sleeping pills were the only way to control this suffering. I completed my graduation with this problem and no one knew about it. After my graduation, I was idle for few months. I had time to prepare for my post-graduation entrance exam. During this time, I also did some research on the problem I had. It was then I came to know that what I was going through was called 'panic attack' and the only way to treat this problem was by visiting a psychiatrist. I also read that this problem may get worse if it did not receive treatment on time. I was stalling this from the past two years. I was too scared after I read about the problem and the consequences. I started to look for alternatives.

The only solution I could think of was leaving the country. I thought it'd help if I stayed in a new environment for some time. I gave my entrance exam MAT, and

I also wrote the GMAT, to help me get admission abroad. I worked really hard and managed to crack both the MAT and GMAT. Finally I managed to score decent scores in both the tests. Now I had to decide on where to go?

I was very confused and started prioritising things for myself. I wanted to travel, see places and meet different people. I went to an International Education Consultancy and they gave me many options, but I chose three countries – Canada, Germany and New Zealand. My priority was to study in a place which was remote and adventurous. I applied in around 20 universities, apart from the universities in India. I waited for a month and I got the conditional offer letters from 13 universities. Education in Canada was very expensive and it was out of my budget. I was left with two options – Germany and New Zealand. I did research from my end about the universities which had offered me a seat, but I was more attracted towards New Zealand. I had an offer from one of the universities in New Zealand which I liked the most because of the city in which the college was. It was in Invercargill. Invercargill is one of the southernmost cities in the world. It seemed calm and empty and this place was perfect for someone like me at that moment. I used to browse through pictures of the roads on the Internet and sometimes I would check that city through *Google Earth*. I was very excited and kept this excitement to myself. I replied to their offer letter and told them that I was interested in taking up the course.

Apart from that, I also applied to a few colleges here in India. After a few days, I received an offer letter with the admission and fee details. First, they wanted me to go through the medical test for my visa formalities and I had to take one more language test, IELTS. I got the medical tests done immediately and also took the IELTS test. While I was going through all the test formalities, my parents were unaware of what I was doing. I had a strong feeling that they would be happy to know about my success. I had my medical results in hand and the only thing I needed now was an educational loan. I collected brochures from banks and every bank asked for some collateral or property documents for the loan. Now it was time when I had to involve my parents in this. I had to tell them about my plans. My Dad was out of town then. I gave him a call and told him that I had received an offer from New Zealand for my post-graduation and I needed to talk to him about it. He sounded happy and informed me that he would be back in a few days and then we could discuss about this. I was very happy to see things falling in place. So finally, I could start a new life. I still didn't tell anything to Mom. I thought she'd freak out if she came to know about all this.

My Mom is a typically emotional woman who cries for small reasons and her life wouldn't work out without my Dad. She was a teacher for a few years but she quit teaching to take on domestic responsibility. I couldn't tell my sister either as she had her final semester exams.

One day I came home later than usual. My Dad was back by then. We had dinner together and he had already informed about my plans to study abroad to my Mom. I could see her already contorted face. We finished dinner and my Dad said, "Jako! Why didn't you tell your Mom about New Zealand?"

"I was waiting for you to get back, Dad," I said.

I didn't know the tragedy would strike the next moment. My Mom started crying as if someone had died. All she said was, "Please don't go."

I didn't know what to do; I just went inside my room, popped a sleeping pill and slept. Next morning, I knew everything was over and Mom wouldn't let me go. I still tried my best to convince her by all means, but she didn't agree to anything.

She said, "Your sister will get married and she'll leave us. You are the only support we have."

I got the point and didn't argue much. And that's how my plan of going abroad came to an end. I was depressed for a few days and finally joined a good college in Bangalore, just like my parents wanted. I would have gone abroad by forcing them, but I knew my Mom would sit and cry every day. And I was too weak to carry the guilt of making my mother cry because of me.

By God's grace, I didn't get any panic attacks after that but I couldn't sleep enough in my post-graduation days. I hardly slept for four to five hours in a day. In my second year, I got hired by an advertising company through campus recruitment from my college. My parents were happy as everything was going according to their wish, but I got addicted to sleeping pills. I used to go and visit a doctor once a month, complaining sleeplessness and he would prescribe me sleeping pills to be taken for two days, but I always used to misuse it. I would go to at least 10 pharmacy stores with the same prescription and stock up pills for a month.

After my post-graduation, I started working in an advertising company and that's where I met Deepa. Our so-called similarities brought us closer and we started dating after a month we met. I thought she was the best thing that ever happened to me. We shared all our troubles and thoughts. We didn't plan our future or marriage, but we had a commitment that we would be together and we wouldn't leave each other, no matter what happened. I suddenly stopped taking sleeping pills; I don't know what magic spell she had, but it worked. Whenever I couldn't get sleep, she used to speak to me the entire night over the phone. Sometimes I would get up in the middle of the night due to some nightmare. I would just give her a call and she was always there for me. I worked in that advertising company for six months and changed my job as my profile got better. Deepa continued working in the same company.

I can't believe that I considered her to be my soul-mate; she was my whole world. I could think nothing but about her all the time. But right now, I feel like I should look for a grave-mate instead of a soul-mate. Losing her suddenly and the pain she inflicted upon me is just indescribable. It only added rocket fuel to my restless and troubled soul. After she left, I had all the time to think on what mattered and what didn't. Panic attacks were back again and I couldn't handle myself anymore. So I went to a psychiatrist. I was asked to go through a cognitive behaviour therapy for a few months as I was diagnosed with something called 'dysthymia'. But I think, I was going through something worse than that. I could not blame the doctor for this. She was just doing her job and helping me to recuperate with her input which I would allow her to give. Honestly I don't know what I wanted from life and every road I thought of was leading to a dead end. I stopped going to work and took some time out for myself. I think I did a right thing or I wouldn't have experienced what I experienced today.

I am working as a project management associate in an IT company. For an outsider, or for someone who doesn't know me, my life may look absolutely perfect. I have a good job, good education, a nice car and a family. What more can anybody ask for? Today, when I had the panic attack, I thought I am back to the same old despicable circumstance, but there was something else in store for me. After the incident, I noticed, I had a strong feeling that everything has a reason. *Yes, everything happens for a reason…*

I fell asleep and suddenly got up at 4 a.m. when a choking feeling engulfed me. I switched on all the lights. I suppose I wanted to make sure that I was still alive. I tried a lot to sleep after that, but I couldn't. I felt as if time was running out of my hand. I stayed up and time just passed away and it was 5 in the morning. I again spent a sleep-deprived night, but this was different from the other usual nights.

It was a Tuesday morning, I decided to go for a morning walk. I saw school children waiting for their buses and old people reading newspapers. Everything looked normal and I couldn't associate myself with anything. I had this 'being different' feeling. I can't believe I literally cried when I walked back home.

I came back and took a cold shower. I thought of meeting my psychiatrist and telling her the whole situation, but I was in no mood to take her positive energy lecture. I wanted to get out of the city for a few days or weeks. I wanted to fix myself before someone would again burden me with a load of crap.

Can I be fixed if I go somewhere? Is there a promised land for me?

Again, I was confused and had a mind block. My Dad was up and he was reading a newspaper that morning. I walked up to him and sat on the chair next to his.

He looked at me and said, "How come you are up so early today? And how is everything at your office?"

"Everything is fine, Dad. I have to go to Chennai for training and I have to leave today." My lie was just spontaneous. I can't believe it came out of my mouth.

"Oh that's why you got up so early today, uh? How long you have to be there? And when are you returning?"

He asked me so many questions as if my presence would make any difference here.

Anyway, I told him it would take two to three weeks.

"What is it regarding?" he asked.

"Training, Dad! On our new project."

I think I convinced him pretty well. He agreed and said, "Did you tell your Mom?"

"No Dad, I tried calling her, but I couldn't go through the call." One more lie.

"It's too hot in Chennai during these times. Get back as soon as you finish your training."

Parents have their own reasons to worry about and they would stop at nothing. I still couldn't believe how I bluntly lied on my Dad's face. Now, I had to leave for somewhere and I had no choice. But where can I go? Should I take someone's advice? Honestly I have no close friends these days. I stopped meeting people from the past two years because I had Deepa with me; actually I ditched them all because of her. The only people I talk to these days are my colleagues at office, and that too, related to work.

4
The Bewilderment

I started going through my cell-phone contacts in order to seek advice from some reliable source. I saw Varun's name; he was my schoolfriend. And the last time when I met him, I remember he was working with a travel company. I never called him in the last three years. I didn't even know if his old number existed. Still I dialled and to my relief it rang.

He picked up the call and said, "Hey Jakooo…what's up man? Long time…"

I couldn't believe that he had my number.

"Hey buddy, I am good. How come you have my number?" I asked.

"The same way you have mine," he said laughingly.

"I want to catch up, buddy, if you are free today?" I said.

"Sure man, we can catch up. What's the scene?" he asked.

"Nothing much. I am planning a vacation, so needed your help. Are you still working in the same place?"

"Yeah! It's been four years and what about you?" he asked.

"I changed my job, man... long story. I'll tell you more when we meet. I am free today. Let me know if we can meet."

"Sure, why don't you come to my office during lunch time?" he said.

His office was close by I told him I would be there by lunch time. My Dad would have a series of questions if I didn't leave today. I had to decide a place to go. It was around one in the afternoon when I reached Varun's office. We went out for lunch. He took me to a Chinese restaurant nearby. I was in no mood to have a happy chit-chat lunch and I couldn't tell everything to Varun either. I pretended like everything was normal and had a normal conversation.

"So Jako, long time buddy. What's up with you? How's life?"

It's a tough question to answer. I didn't know where to begin from.

"Everything is fine, buddy; just need a long break from this hectic work schedule."

"That's nice. Where do you wan'na go? Got any places in mind?"

"I am just blank, bro. Just tell me a place where I can relax for a few days."

"Relax, what do you want to do? Girlfriend issues?"

"I don't have any girlfriend, dude; just need some time for myself. You know any place where I can be myself and relax for some time?"

"You want to go abroad, I can suggest some kick ass places."

"No man, somewhere here; not abroad."

"Hill-stations or beaches? Or you want to explore some city?"

"Beach would be fine; I am not much of a hill-station person."

"Have you ever been to Goa?"

"No."

"Do one thing – I have got a few friends there from my college. I can hook you up. Stay there as long as you want."

"That's not a bad idea. I have never been there and I have heard a lot about Goa. Yeah, I am fine with it."

"So, how many of you are going?"

"Just me," I said.

"Just you? What's wrong with you, Jako? Is everything alright?"

"Would something go wrong if you have to travel alone? Or they won't welcome a single traveller in Goa?"

Varun laughed and said, "You'll never change, man."

What more could I tell him. A guy like him, who was happy with his job and womanising skills, can never understand what I was going through. He could never think about things deeply and he was happy as long as his job paid him well, and wouldn't mind having new girlfriends every six month. I pity myself for being an emotional fool. Anyway, Goa did not sound an ideal place to visit at this point of time. Since I didn't have any other place in mind, it's better to consider Varun's suggestion. At least I had a place to go now. I made up my mind and backing off would be the foolest thing to do.

I finished my lunch and on my way back home, I kept wondering about my job. I had a strong urge to quit the job instantly and run away. But I had worked there for almost one-and-a-half years and I would end up jeopardising my experience letter if I did so. One-and-a-half years of experience was too much to lose. My manager kept calling me since the day I stopped going to the office because I had disappeared from there without any prior notice. I didn't answer any of his calls and now I would have to make up a story to tell him.

I reached home and called my manager on his cell phone. I thought he would burst out with anger but he was cool and asked me, "What's wrong, Jackson? Where are you? Why didn't you answer my calls and why haven't you turned up at office since last week?"

Again there were too many "whys" for me to answer. I couldn't tell him much and I just said, "I ran into some trouble, Amit. It's an emergency and I need some more time. Like, two to three weeks more. I am very confused about something."

"Are you planning to quit?" he asked.

"I am not sure about that too. I'll be out of town for a few weeks and I'll certainly meet you once I get back," I said.

He didn't ask any more questions after that and said "It's okay Jackson. Call me once you are back."

I was glad that he understood and approved the leave. I didn't had to worry about my work anymore.

After I spoke to my manager, I started packing my belongings. I stuffed as many clothes as I could in the bag and also took my laptop along as my Dad would become suspicious if I left my laptop behind. After all, you have to think a lot before fooling a police officer.

Varun called me to check if I had booked the tickets. I told him that I was driving. He freaked out and said, "Are you crazy, Jako? You wan'na drive all the way to Goa, that too all alone? You know how far it is? It'll take almost 10 to 12 hours."

"Don't worry, man, I can drive. You just speak to your friend there and let me know."

"You've gone crazy, man. Okay I'll speak to him and give you a call," Varun said.

Have I gone crazy? Even I thought that I had gone crazy, but crazy people wouldn't know that they are crazy.

They think they are doing something sane. Never mind, I did some research over the Internet about the distance and road map. Varun was wrong. I could reach there in eight to ten hours at the max. I took the printout of the road-map and I was all set for my journey.

It was 4 p.m. Varun called me and said that he had spoken to his friend there and his name was Michael, who had his own restaurant there. Varun gave me Michael's cell number and asked me to call him before I left, so that he could come and meet me the next day. I thanked Varun for the help and packed the other left-out items.

I took my car to the service station to ensure everything was fine. The mechanic ran a quick check to make sure that everything was fixed. I asked him to change the engine oil. After that I went to the filling station and got my fuel tank filled. I came back home for dinner. Since Mom was not at home, Dad asked me to order food from some restaurant for dinner. I had dinner with Dad and after finishing it, I loaded the luggage in the car. My Dad asked me why I was taking the car.

I again lied, saying, "I am going to park the car in office."

"Why? Can't you leave it at home?" he asked.

"I am getting picked up from the office and it'll be convenient for me to get back if I reach here at night, when I return." I again fibbed coolly.

"Okay, call me when you get time," he said.

I left home at around 9:30 p.m., and called Michael, I suppose Varun had already given him my number. As soon as he picked the call, he said, "Hey, you are Varun's friend, right?"

"Yeah! This is Jackson," I said.

"So you are leaving tonight?"

"Yes, I'll reach there by tomorrow morning."

"Okay, give me a call when you reach here," he said.

I spoke to Michael and drove straight to that graveyard; the gates were locked. I stood there for some time, and started recalling yesterday's event. It was all dark inside and there were a few dim yellow lights inside the cemetery. Anyway, who needs lights over there? I kind of thanked myself for being there yesterday and moved on, as I had to drive for a long time. Honestly, I was thankful for what I had gone through. I should have experienced it long time back; anyway better late than never.

5

A Journey without Milestones

Bangalore is one of the most crowded cities in India and when it comes to traffic, it tops the list. Almost everyone has a vehicle here. By the time I crossed the city, it was 11 p.m. Finally, I hit the highway, thinking how could things change so quickly? Until yesterday, I was cribbing about my girlfriend, my job and my life. But now, nothing seemed important anymore.

Gone were those days when I used to drive on highways at top speed, savouring every bit of driving. My mind used to be blank and I would be lost in moments without any thoughts, but now, only God could understand my condition. I again let my random thoughts take control of my personality. Whenever I wish to take a detour from these sick thoughts, my mind works otherwise it is as if this phenomenon has no control. All the tools, methods, medications and God knows what all had failed to fix this problem of mine. Or maybe I was using only one tool over and over again.

And who says that you can't rewind the moments of your life? I don't know if it's a boon or a curse, but I have a potential to recall each and every moment of my life whenever I want to. And when I am in retrospection, few things of past make me feel like I am a failure and few moments give me a heroic feeling. But I still keep recalling them to convince my soul that I too had an existence at some point of time in my life.

I wish I could hallucinate and create someone who would help me unburden all my worries. But the truth is, I don't want to be happy anymore. Not because of the sadness that comes after that; just because the sadness lasts for a long time.

My first stop was at a coffee shop, 70 kms away from Bangalore, and that was the only place where I halted during my journey for refreshment. As I remember, I dozed off a couple of times while driving because my head was heavy as I had not slept from the last two days. The journey wasn't that tiring and I reached Panaji in nine hours as anticipated. I reached Goa around 9 a.m. and I was starving. My back was aching because I had been sitting in a single posture from the past nine hours.

Weather in Goa was not that pleasant; I could feel the humidity early in the morning. I rushed into a restaurant to freshen up. It felt rejuvenating when I splashed some cool water on the tired, sweaty face and hands. As expected, the breakfast menu was full of options. There were many dishes on the menu card and which I had never eaten before. I thought of trying a new delicacy for a change, but dismissed the idea and ordered the normal breakfast.

I finished the breakfast and came out to call Michael. I was about to light a cigarette when Michael called, "Hey Jackson, did you reach?"

"Yeah I reached, about an hour ago."

"Why didn't you call me then? Looks like you want to explore Goa all on your own?"

"No, I don't have that plan. I am in Panaji now. Will you come?"

"Sure, give me the address."

I gave Michael the restaurant's address. He said he would be here in 30 minutes. Car's engine had cooled down to normal. I wiped the windshield in the meantime; after that I sat in the car and started smoking. As promised, Michael was there in 30 minutes. The moment I saw him, I had no doubt that he was indeed Varun's friend. He was a dark looking guy, a wannabe rapper type. He was wearing a blue shiny t-shirt which was three times his size; it was almost touching his knees. He was wearing a tilted cap and wore a long and heavy set chain around his neck, just the kind the rappers wore. His eyebrows were pierced.

I was sitting in the car. Michael came straight up to me without giving a search around the place. He came to the window and said, “Hey, you are Jackson right?”

“Yes, it’s me.”

He sat in the car and asked me, “Where would you like to stay?”

I told him I was relying on him and would go by his suggestion as this was my first visit to Goa. He looked at me with a strange expression and said, “This is the first time you’ve come to Goa?”

“Yeah, I wanted to come here from my high school days but never got a chance,” I said.

“There’s no place like this, man; you can do whatever you want here. And now for the stay, you have two options. You can stay near the beach in a shack or you can stay in a hotel here in Panaji.”

I thought staying near the beach would be nice and asked him to take me to the beach shacks.

“It is holiday season and the chances of getting a shack is less,” he said. There were around 10 beaches in Goa, and he would take me to five-six of them, so that I could check the shacks. I was fine with the idea of staying near the beach.

I asked Michael, “Which way to drive first?”

Michael suggested the Calangute beach where he had his restaurant. Calangute beach was around 15 kms away from Panaji.

"It'll take 30 minutes to reach as the roads are narrow," he said.

We headed towards Calangute beach and Michael asked me why I had come alone?

"I wanted to travel all alone by myself; wanted to explore new places undisturbed. So I packed my bag and drove all the way to Goa alone," I said beaming.

Michael laughed and said, "There are lots of things you will do for the first time in Goa. By the way how do you know Varun?"

"I know him since school days when we studied together for seven years," I answered.

"Wow, that's nice. It's good to have school friends around. They have a clear idea about you."

"I really don't think they have any clear idea about us. They are one of those people who have seen you growing up. And eventually everyone is bound to leave you sooner or later or you may have to leave everything all of a sudden."

"What do you mean?" Michael asked.

"You know if you happen to die suddenly, you may not even get a chance to say goodbye to anyone."

"You think too much Jackson. There is a lot of time to worry about all these things. We should think about this when we are really old."

I smiled at him and said, "Yeah, you are right."

I think I crossed the line with him; he wasn't the kind of guy who would be interested in listening to any psychedelic bullshit of mine. We both were silent for some time and I was driving quietly. Michael pulled a coupon from his pocket and said, "Hey Jackson, there is a party tonight and my friends have organised it. I got passes; would you like to come along? We will have an awesome time."

"Thanks, dude but I am sorry, I can't make it today. I need to rest tonight since the last couple of days have been very tiring for me."

"That's completely fine," he kept back the pass inside his pocket and shrugged casually.

Actually, it was not about me being tired. I don't like going to night parties; the loud music with flashing lights in the darkness makes me go crazy. I feel suffocated. I hardly go to any parties; a couple or so if I calculate.

We reached Michael's restaurant. I parked my car there and unloaded my luggage. We had a cold drink and a smoke. Michael introduced me to few of his friends there and left me with them because he had to take care of some business. He told me that he'd be back in some time. It was shocking for his friends when they came to know that I was there all by myself. I talked to them for some time, amidst which we exchanged casual information about each other. Few of them were in college and others were having jobs. I asked them if I could get a calm and silent place to stay for a few days.

They all laughed and said, "It's not a good time to visit Goa if you are looking for peace of mind. Everything is crowded here, from beaches to hotels."

I had still placed some hope on Michael; I was expecting him to arrange a place for me. Michael returned from his work and I went to him and said, "Hey I was speaking to your friends and they all said it's hard to get a place in the holiday season."

"Don't worry, man, I'll hook you up," Michael said.

Michael sounded pretty confident, which obviously induced me and I kept my spirits high. We left Michael's restaurant to take a short tour of the place. He had a motorbike, which he had modified into a chopper bike. We set out in search of an accommodation. We started with the nearest Calangute beach and covered almost all the beaches in Goa for the shacks.

To my dismay, we couldn't find even one shack, available. Everyone said a flat 'no' on our faces. It was disappointing as we returned without any positive result. I was famished, which made my head spin. I asked Michael to take me to some restaurant for lunch. I told him we could think of some other alternatives after lunch. Michael took me to his restaurant and I ate a sumptuous lunch.

There were minimal chances of getting a shack. Michael said, "It's a bad time to be in Goa. You should have told me a few weeks earlier as I would have made some arrangements."

I told him that my trip was not pre-planned.

Seriously, who knew I would end up burying an old lady?

Michael asked me if I wanted to check few hotels.

"What other options we have?" I asked.

"We can try service apartments. They'll be more comfortable compared to hotels. What say?"

"Sure, I am okay with that," I said.

He took me to a place which was at walking distance from his restaurant. It was a huge bungalow, which had three-four small apartments on the top. I liked it instantly, after having a look and immediately told Michael that I was ready to take it.

"Chill, man, we need to check if it is available first."

We went inside and there was an old man sitting behind the reception. Michael spoke to him in their local language and asked him if there was any apartment available. The old man told him they had only one available towards the end of the corridor which got vacant in the morning. We were running on good luck.

I came forward and said, "We will take it sir. How much is it?" Michael looked at me and said, "You look like you are in real hurry, man. What are you planning to do?"

"Nothing much, Michael. I just need to sleep. I haven't slept properly from the past few days. You have no idea how tired I am."

"Are you sure, you don't want to check out some more places?"

"No, I like this place. I am fine with it," I replied.

I actually liked the place as it was surrounded by coconut trees, and it looked like a perfectly peaceful place. We went back to Michael's restaurant where I picked up my luggage. Michael gave me a helping hand. Actually he was very helpful in all the matters. After shifting to the apartment, I called Varun and told him everything.

I thought to take a shower and change my clothes, but sleep wouldn't let me do anything. I just crashed the moment I saw the clean bed. I zoned out for I don't know how long. I woke up when my phone started ringing. It was my Dad calling to check if I had reached Chennai. I lied to him and said, "I was sleeping after I came from office."

I switched on all the lights and it was 10:30 p.m. I was again hungry and I didn't know what would I get to eat at this time. I called Michael to check if there was any restaurant open at this hour.

"Welcome to Goa, my friend. The day starts at night here," he said.

I don't know what he meant but I think he said I still had my dinner chances.

I took a hot bath and it took away all my tiredness. I changed my clothes to something comfortable and walked down. I went to Michael's restaurant. He was sitting with a few of his friends and they were all having beer. Michael asked me to join them.

"I quit drinking," I said.

"What are you saying? You are not going to drink ever again?" he asked.

"I don't know about forever not drinking, but I am trying to quit and I haven't consumed alcohol since the past few months."

"I admire your will power, Jackson," he said.

I asked him for a menu card, so that I could order dinner. The real reason for giving up drinking was Deepa.

After she left, I drank continuously for days to get rid of her memories. But after drinking I used to recall everything that I wanted to forget.

I finished dinner at Michael's restaurant and asked him directions to get to the beach. He suggested me to take the straight road and I would reach the beach in 10 minutes by foot. I asked Michael if I could take his motorbike. I was too lazy to walk after the heavy dinner. He gave his motorbike and said that I could hire a motorbike on rent if I wanted.

I set off on Michael's motorbike. I didn't go to the beach. I went towards the main market as I thought of exploring places by myself. I went to Panaji again and filled petrol in Michael's motorbike and started roaming in the city.

The city was more beautiful than I had thought it would be; it still had the Portuguese essence in it. The wide roads and old churches were mesmerising. I traversed the whole city at night; shops and restaurants were open till late night. There were no traffic signals and no cops to catch. I reached a beach, which was close to Panaji city. I couldn't know the name of the beach as there was no one around. I sat there for some time; it was so silent that I could hear nothing but the sound of the waves. While I was sitting, a man came up to me and started talking loudly in the local language. I couldn't understand anything, but he was so drunk that he was not able to stand properly. He started waving his hand for some reason. It didn't look alright; I started the motorbike and left the place.

There was a wide road parallel to the beach, which went straight to I don't know where. I just took off on that and after 2-3 kms, there was a residential area with a lane full of bungalows.

And there were concrete benches by the footpaths; these benches resembled the ones I saw at the cemetery back in Bangalore. I stopped and sat on one of the benches. I could see the beach from where I was sitting. There was a gentle cool breeze flowing which soothed my anxiousness. Two days back at this exact moment, I was lying on my bed and cribbing about life's failures and today I was sitting here with a whole new perspective on things. The only thing I regretted was the time I had wasted chasing and worrying about things which didn't really matter any more. But, I don't know how many Jako's like me were chasing the same thing and setting material goals. I was glad about whatever had happened to me; it was an eye opener. I wished I could share it with someone. My phone started ringing and it was Michael; he wanted to know where I was.

"I am in Panaji, sitting on the beach," I said.

"Why don't you come back to the restaurant?"

"Do you need the bike?" I asked.

"No man, we are having fun here. Why don't you join us?"

I thought of going back and joining them if they were really having fun apart from drinking. I left the place and headed back to Michael's restaurant. On the way, I was bit confused on which road to take, but still I made it.

I reached there and it looked like they were having some kind of a house party. I went inside and found Michael. I gave him the bike's key. He introduced me to a few other people, but what grabbed my attention was a group of people sitting in a semi-circle in the lawn, with a guy sat in the middle and talking to them. He was in his late forties and he was wearing a yellow coloured *kurta* which had OM printed all over. I went close and sat at the back. He was talking something about meditation. Everyone was listening to him carefully, but I couldn't catch everything that he was saying due to the loud music being played somewhere around. I don't know from how long he was talking, I was there at the end of his lecture. After he finished talking, he looked at me and said, "I am sorry, I haven't seen you before." Everybody turned and looked at me.

"I came here today. I am Michael's friend," I said.

"Oh okay, you are Michael's friend. Where are you from?"

"Bangalore," I said.

Everyone got up and left. Even he smiled at me and said, "Will see you later."

I wished I could hear more of his talk. The topic was really interesting on which he was talking about. I went back inside, looking for Michael, but I couldn't find him anywhere. May be he was busy somewhere. It was 2 a.m. and I started feeling drowsy. I thought of calling it a day and came back to the apartment and slept.

6
Leap of Faith

Next morning I woke up early and went to see Michael, but he was not at his restaurant. I thought of going to the beach by myself. Before reaching the beach, on the way I saw a board saying 'motorbikes on rent' at an ice cream shop. I stopped and checked a few motorbikes. All they needed was a copy of my driver's licence and an initial deposit amount. I rented a motorbike which gave maximum fuel efficiency as per that shop guy. After hiring the bike, I sped towards the beach to have my breakfast. The beach was deserted during this hour of the day. I think people prefer to rise up late here. I again opted for the normal breakfast at the restaurant I always preferred it over oily food.

After I finished my breakfast, I walked up to the beach and sat on the simmering golden sand, lost in my own thoughts, amidst which the makeshift vendor approached, asking me to buy his products which ranged from body massage to wooden necklace and bracelets.

One good thing about these vendors was they don't trouble you if you say 'no' politely with a smile. I always smiled at them and said a, 'no'.

A couple came and sat next to me and the girl constantly kept staring at me. May be she recognised me from somewhere or she was up to something dubious. I pitied her boyfriend! What an unlucky soul.

It reminded me of an incident. Once I was having lunch with Deepa in a restaurant and there were two guys sitting on the other table. Deepa told me that one of them was staring at her. First I asked her to ignore them and then something struck me and I asked her, "How do you know they are staring at you?"

She replied, saying that because I saw him staring at me. You see, it all started because she saw him and he ganged a potential opportunity!

I know the fact that men and women are biologically different and even our brains differ from each other considerably, but can't we be at least little similar on an emotional level? Is there no such thing as loyalty or trust anymore?

What more can I say? I thought my relationship with Deepa was inseparable, but since I have no control over the ravages of time, I was forced to accept whatever came in my fate. Anyway, I was not interested in them. I was trying to get a feel of the new place and I was bent on seeing everything with a fresh outlook and enjoy as much as I could. But, no matter what I tried to do, an unfamiliar guilt was kicking me from inside. It was like by the end of every thought I ended up thinking a miserable thing and finished every sentence with a miserable word.

I am sure that this question had passed in every mind and it was very simple.

If there is any God in the near vicinity, is it not his responsibility to take care of us and answer to our prayers when we call upon? Is there no way that we can talk to him directly? After all, he claims to be our creator. Oh man, these godly things are so not convincing.

I finished with my loneliness and called Michael. He was at the restaurant. I asked him whether he was free, so that we could meet up. He was free till afternoon. Actually I wanted to know about the guy who was sitting and talking in the lawn last night. I went to Michael's restaurant and he was busy cleaning his motorbike.

"Oh, you hired a motorbike?" he said.

"Yeah, I hired it this morning. Where were you last night? I came looking for you inside but I couldn't find you."

"May be I was in the backyard; I was completely sloshed last night. What happened? Why were you looking for me?" he asked.

"It wasn't too important. I happened meet a guy last night. He was talking to a few of your friends in the lawn. I think he was in late forties. I was just curious and didn't get to speak to him much."

"Oh, you must be talking about Shankar."

"I don't know. I didn't get his name," I said.

"Was he wearing a *kurta* and had a pony?"

"Yes exactly!"

"His name is Shankar; he comes here very often. He stays nearby and teaches meditation; he also conducts classes on that. Did you speak to him last night?" Michael asked.

"Yes I did. He asked me where I am from, but I couldn't speak much to him."

"Hey! He conducts crash courses. If you are interested, you can go and ask him about it. By the way, how long are you planning to stay here?"

"One or two weeks, or may be less. I haven't decided anything on that yet," I said.

"So, why don't you meet Shankar and check if he has any courses for you?"

It wasn't a bad idea, I heard Shankar talking on some motivational subject last night. Somehow, I realised that I was being utterly pessimistic towards life and could end up doing things which I shouldn't be doing. May be he can help me with some of my constraints.

I asked Michael to take me to Shankar's place.

"Looks like you are in a hurry to take admission," he said.

"Will he be available now?" I asked.

"Yes I think so." Michael finished his work and took me to Shankar's place. Shankar lived the next road, so we took a stroll. And while walking, I asked Michael whether he is happy with his life, his job and himself.

"You mean my work here? Yes, I am happy about it."

"No. Are you happy with everything? I mean with your life?"

"What strange question is that? Of course I am happy. I have everything that I need. This is my Dad's restaurant which I have inherited after his death. I renovated it and I am planning to extend it more."

"Your Dad must be proud of you then."

"I don't know. He worked hard all his life for the restaurant."

"Yeah, that's what I was about to tell you. No matter how hard we work to create and build things, we have to leave it back here," I said.

"Hey, what's the problem with you? You always seem to come down to these death talks?" he asked.

"Death talks?"

"Yeah, you have been talking about these things since yesterday. Has anyone close to you died?"

"No, I was just talking generally."

"Everyone will die one day, dude, so don't think of that and trouble yourself. Just chill."

I could not say anything more to Michael. I don't blame him; it's common with everyone. People are afraid to talk about the only end that is most certain. They are uncertain about the only certainty. I wonder, what would go wrong if we would at least try to see and think differently? I don't think there's any commandment saying. 'Thou shall not think differently.'

We reached Shankar's place and rang the doorbell. He stayed on the first floor. Shankar opened the door and was excited to see Michael. I think they knew each other pretty well. We went inside and his walls were painted in different colours and had tribal art. Michael introduced me to Shankar and Shankar instantly remembered that we had met last night. On the second floor, he had a big hall where he conducted his classes. Shankar seemed to be an outspoken person and was very enthusiastic about everything he was talking about. I thought my visit to Goa didn't go in vain. At least I'll get to do something purposeful. Shankar informed that he had done many courses in meditation and yoga and a few of the disciples were from foreign institutes. He was fluent in many languages and even his English was pretty decent. While I was checking Shankar's impressive certificates displayed on the wall of his office, Michael came to me and said he would leave as he had an important business to take care of. We decided to meet in the evening.

Shankar took to me to the second floor. There was a big hall with a raised platform attached to which was his small office.

He took me his cabin and said, "This is my small office."

We sat and I asked him about the programs that he conducted and activities he was involved in. Shankar said, "He was staying in Goa from the past two years and before that he was an independent trainer and a school teacher."

I didn't ask anything about his family or where he was from. But, he was interested in knowing things about me; he wanted to know everything about me. I told him about my job, my educational background and a little about my family, and things I could tell to a stranger. Finally after curbing his initial curiosity, he asked me, why I had come to Goa all alone?

"I was distressed and needed a break for myself," I simply replied.

"So you are here to rediscover yourself?" he asked.

I had no idea what was he talking about, I simply said a 'no' and he didn't ask anything more.

But I asked myself, 'Do people actually travel to rediscover themselves? Is this the reason I am travelling?' I didn't feel like discussing much with Shankar at that moment because that was our first meeting.

"It's lunch time. I usually have lunch at Michael's restaurant. Would you like to join me?" Shankar asked.

"Sure, even I was planning to go there," I said.

We both went to Michael's restaurant for lunch. On the way, I asked more about his courses and he gave me a rough idea. Michael wasn't there in the restaurant, so we sat outside in the lawn to have our lunch. I didn't want to share anything personal with him, but I asked Shankar about the meditation and how can it helps someone who is distressed both physically and mentally.

"When do you get more tired, Jackson?" he asked.

"While working," I said.

"Okay, if it is a work-related problem. We have to deal separately, for example. Your body may get tired from sitting for long hours at the same place and at the same time your mind gets tired of doing the same job for long hours."

"Do you exercise?" he asked.

"No," I replied.

"See, that's where the problems exist. All our internal organs are programmed in such a way that they are in constant motion like our external organs. And if we don't maintain our external body in the right way, we may have both mental and physical problems."

I interrupted in between and asked him if there was any way to avoid the thoughts which came repeatedly, and if there was any way to divert myself whenever I got these unnecessary thoughts.

"What thoughts are you talking about?" he asked.

"Just the random thoughts about something bad that has happened," I said.

I couldn't elaborate my problem in front of him because he was a yoga teacher, not a psychiatrist. He thought for a while and said, "I can teach you a small meditation technique to start with. It takes about two to three minutes and it will be very effective for what you are asking for."

"Sit straight at a place and close your eyes. Take deep breaths three-four times and start observing everything that is happening around you. Listen to every sound and start focusing on everything that you hear, and continue this three-four times and slowly open your eyes by taking deep breaths. In this way, your mind's attention will be diverted to something other than yourself. And its impact will disconnect you from unnecessary thoughts."

"What do you call this?"

"It is one of the Zen Mindful Meditation techniques," he said.

"Are you a Buddhist?"

"I am multi-religious Jackson. I believe in Jesus too," he smiled.

After some time he got a phone call and he had to leave. I took his cell number and told him that I may call later.

After he left, I closed my eyes and tried the technique he had taught me. There was no noise around me and I couldn't practice it appropriately. I decided to try this at the beach. In the evening I took a walk to the beach. It had been ages and I hadn't seen the sunset. I reached the beach and it was more crowded than I had expected it to be. I wanted to try the technique there. I walked further to a deserted part of the beach and sat on a flat surface. I closed my eyes and took deep breaths. I could hear the waves, people screaming from the paraglider and all what was happening around. I couldn't check the time but I opened my eyes after a few minutes. It worked exactly the way he said. I couldn't think of anything related to me. But when I opened my eyes, everything was back again, like the way it was. It was just a distraction technique, not the solution. I could probably use it when things would get worse. This just made me forget the reality for some time.

The sun turned orange and it looked like it was going to melt in some time and so it did in a few minutes. Slowly people started moving from the beach. I am sure everyone had a plan for their evening, unlike me. My cell started ringing and it was my manager from office, I didn't answer his call. I wasn't in a mood to listen to any office story. I thought of going to Panaji for dinner. So I went back to Michael's restaurant to pick up my motorbike. Michael was back and he asked me how my day went and what did I do with Shankar. I told him the whole story. I asked Michael if he could come with me to Panaji. But, he said he was waiting for Shankar.

"Why are you waiting for him?" I queried.

"Shankar's laptop has crashed; we have to take it to the service station."

I thought of staying back for some time, so that I could tell Shankar about the technique I had tried. I told Michael I would stay back for a while as I wanted to meet Shankar. After some time, Shankar came with his laptop and he was in a hurry to go to the service station. I tried talking to him, but he asked me to meet him after dinner.

Michael was searching for his bike's key and meanwhile he asked Shankar what had happened to the laptop.

Shankar said he had plugged his laptop for charging and he was away for some time and when he came back, the screen was blank. When he tried to restart it, the laptop didn't turn on.

I overheard their conversation and went to Shankar to ask him if the internet was connected, and he said yes. I knew what exactly was wrong with his laptop. While Shankar had kept it for charging, his operating system tried updating itself automatically and he had shut it down before it completed the updates. All I needed to do was boot the system and restore the setting to factory settings. I asked them if they had the external storage, so that I could extract the data. Unfortunately, they didn't have it.

"I can fix your laptop, Mr Shankar," I said.

"Can you?"

"Yes, it is one of the side effects of working in an IT company." They all laughed.

I had an external storage disk back in the apartment. I always carry it around because it has all my music and movies collection. I told them that I would go and fetch it.

"I don't need the data. I just need my system back," Shankar said.

"I am not 100 per cent sure that the data will be recovered but we can give it a try," I said.

Michael thought it was a good idea and he asked me to get my drive. I ran to my apartment and got the drive. As I had predicted, his laptop had the problem I had expected. I turned on the laptop and booted the system and tried to extract the data into my storage drive. It took almost 30 minutes to reset his laptop. Luckily all his 350 GB of data was recovered. Before I restored the settings, I was about to copy the data back in his laptop when the battery died, Shankar said he would take the drive with him and copy it later.

Since I had fixed the laptop, Shankar stayed back at Michael's restaurant. As usual, Michael opened a beer can and we all started chatting. I couldn't ask or talk more about meditation to Shankar as Michael was there. So I changed the topic. They asked me how I was finding Goa and what I had been doing. As we were talking, a few of Michael's friend from the neighbourhood had come over and joined us. We all had our dinner together after which all of them started watching football. My plan for the next day was to go to Panaji and explore the city. I told Michael that I will call him tomorrow and I came back to my apartment and slept soundly.

7
Wildly Shaken

Next morning, I left the apartment early and reached Panaji on my motorbike. After my breakfast, I had plans to explore the whole city. I called Michael to ask him where I should begin from. He gave me a list of places to visit. Out of them, I chose to visit St. Francis Xavier's shrine which rested in the 'Basilica of Bom Jesus'. Among the many praises I have heard about Goa, after the beaches, the next thing that attracted the tourists was the church where the body of St. Francis Xavier was placed. Since, it was difficult to find a living saint anywhere, the best I could do was to visit a dead one.

When I was a kid, my parents tried hard to make me believe in religion, but whenever I thought of strengthening my faith or tried to believe in God, I never sensed any spirituality and always ended up asking myself, why do we need religion? And what difference can any religion make in life.

I took the address from the localities and reached there. The church was in old Goa, which was a 15-minutes ride from Panaji, and I reached there at around 10 a.m. The church was huge, constructed in a Gothic style and was built a few centuries ago. Its ancient and antique look was very magnetising and anyone who saw it for the first time would get the feeling that there is something inside that which you can't ignore and walk away.

On a week day, it was quite early to enter the church. The prayer hall was much bigger than I had assumed, but it was all empty. My voice would have echoed if I had spoken something, I moved around the prayer hall and in the courtyard, but I couldn't find the tomb that I was looking for. After some time, a group of people entered the payer hall. As soon as they entered, almost everyone started clicking pictures of whatever they saw around them. I mean, they didn't see anything from their own eyes first. All they wanted to do was to capture the images to show it to others. It was as if they were travelling and exploring to flaunt it to others. They had a guide along with them and he pointed to the right corner and said, "There is the tomb of St. Francis Xavier." Before the crowd could get there, I rushed to take a quick look.

There was a metal casket in which lay the body of Saint Xavier's. I couldn't see what was inside clearly but overheard people saying that his body was lying horizontal inside. I stood there for some time thinking which of his deeds helped him? What made him the renowned and pious saint which he was? But it proved one point certainly that even great, powerful and pious men cannot escape death.

I came out for a smoke and my random thoughts struck me with their usual traits. For a moment I thought of making a confession as maybe it'll help if I share my problems with a stranger. I went inside the church and tried Shankar's technique. But this time it didn't work at all. While I was trying the meditation, I had this thought running at the back of my mind that all of this, which I was trying to do, was to divert and distract myself from something which I can't face or resolve. I needed to figure out how to deal with life because I had no idea what haunted me and why? Why do I have to always struggle with the decisions I make? I think it's better to go with the flow and accept the things the way they are. I had tears in my eyes and I bowed my head and said, 'If there is any God, please help me. Give me death if it's better for me or spare me with a life worth living.'

Anyway, visiting the church had a good impact. These days, I just need something or anything meaningful which can at least give me a clue about what should I do and what is really important. I planned to go and meet Shankar in the evening. May be I should share my problems with him. Who knows he might have an answer? I came out of the church and clicked a few pictures for myself. It was lunch time and I was very hungry as my appetite was in a good state. I ate as much as I could and set off to see Old Goa.

Old Goa was less commercialised as compared to Panaji or any other place in Goa. I went shopping by foot and bought a few antiques such as old wine bottles and ashtrays before I left.

I rode on the highway and reached Panaji in no time. As soon as I entered the city, I saw a girl who looked exactly like Deepa and all my emotions came flooding back. I knew there was no escape for me today and if I had to escape, intoxication was the only option. I checked out a few bars but all of them were crowded, so I thought of picking up booze from a wine shop and get drunk at my apartment. I thought of inviting Michael. I was sure he wouldn't say no to alcohol. But on my way to the apartment, I saw a small bar which had a nice ambience. I went inside. It wasn't crowded; they were playing blues. After searching for a suitable corner, I finally found a calm place. I started drinking there, as if there was no tomorrow for me. After an hour or two the bartender asked me to leave because they were closing in some time. I was so disturbed that even after drinking so much, I couldn't get high. I paid the bill and walked out, and rode back to the apartment without any trouble. I had no idea where I parked the bike and how I climbed the stairs; all I remembered was crashing on to the bed.

Next morning, Michael came to my apartment at around 10 a.m. I had no idea how long he had been ringing the doorbell. I woke up when he knocked at the window pane. After I opened my eyes, I couldn't lift my head due to the hangover. I felt as if some brick or heavy stone was tied around my head. I opened the door and Michael came inside and said, "What happened to you? Why are you not answering your phone?"

Before I could tell him anything, he looked at me and figured out that I was drunk last night.

"I thought you don't drink. Why didn't you call me yesterday?" he asked.

"I didn't plan to drink Michael. I don't know what happened that I ended up drinking."

"But, why didn't you answer your phone?"

"I left it back here. Why, what happened?" I asked.

"Shankar wanted to know if you took the hard drive after you recovered the data."

"No, I left it at your restaurant," I said.

"Check in your bag; you might have brought it by mistake."

When I checked my bag, I had the drive in it. I don't know how it came there. I told him that I'll give it to Shankar myself later when I'll be meeting him.

"You want me to get you something to eat?" Michael asked.

I told him that I'll sleep for some more time and I'll have lunch later. Michael left and asked me to give him a call if I needed something. After Michael left, I tried to sleep again, but my headache wouldn't let me sleep. I tried for an hour but failed to sleep. I got up and drank a bottle of water and checked my phone. I had 34 missed calls from three people – my Dad, Shankar and my manager. I didn't use the phone after I spoke to Michael in the morning; I just threw it in the bag. These days I got calls only from banks or from some telesales; there was a time when Deepa used to call or message me every hour. And after she left, everything stopped. I wish I hadn't isolated myself from my other friends; I left all of them because of her. But when I think of going back to them now, I feel a pang of guilt at being selfish. I may appear to them as acting on my whims and fancies.

Anyways, I called my manager first and I was sure that he was going to tell me about my job being at stake. But he conveyed something for which I didn't know how to react. He said, they had taken me off the project which I was working on and I will have to wait till the next project starts, and that'll take two more weeks. I didn't know if it was good news or a bad one, but all I could make out from that was that I had an extended vacation of two more weeks. I pretended like it was my loss and wanted to resume work as soon as possible. My manager asked me to take it as a vacation. He had no clue that I was already on one. At least, I didn't lose my job yet.

After that I called Dad but he didn't pick up, so I sent him a message saying '*I am doing fine*'. In the end, I called Shankar, as he had called around 20 times yesterday.

I spoke to him and asked him as to why he called me so many times.

"I needed your hard drive, Jackson. I have some important data in that. Can I come over and collect it from you now?" he asked.

"I'll get it after some time. Are you in your office?"

"No, I am going somewhere. Can I come and collect it now?" he said.

May be there was something he needed urgently, so I asked him to come and collect it. I freshened up and logged into my account to check my mails. Meanwhile, I connected the hard drive to copy a few movies. After copying, I saw a yellow icon on one of Shankar's folder and it was around 300 GB. I thought he had some important stuff related to his work and out of curiosity, I opened the folder.

Now, it was Shankar's turn to come out of the closet.

That folder was filled with porn videos. I was completely flabbergasted; it was mind baffling. I couldn't believe what I saw. It was a sudden disturbance to the mind and how would you react if you saw something like that? A meditation tutor had 300 GB's of porn? What does it prove? It took away my hangover in a fraction of second. So this was the thing he wanted so badly for which he had called me numerous times yesterday? I pushed the laptop aside and lighted a cigarette.

I thought of deleting everything from the hard drive and telling him that the hard drive crashed, but what difference would that make? He'll go back and collect it again. I was amazed to see his other side. All this time, I was planning to share my problems with him and considered him to be someone who was capable of helping me. But now, I started doubting his capabilities and achievements in his trade.

After a few minutes, Shankar arrived and knocked at the door. I opened it with anger, and thought of yelling at him '*get lost*' and bang the door on his face. Since I had discovered his fakeness now, I wanted to see how well he managed it. He came inside as usual with a smile on his face and asked with politeness, "Where were you yesterday? I tried calling you."

"I was in Old Goa."

"Oh! Good, how was it and what did you do?"

"Nothing much, visited the churches and did some shopping."

"That's nice, you should go to churches more often," he smiled.

What could be worse? A pervert was advising me to approach God. I felt like throwing that hard drive on his face. But then, dealing with him politely for the last time would be the right thing to do. I handed him the hard drive and said, "I am going out for some work."

"Oh, even I am on my way to somewhere. Thanks for helping me with recovering the data."

He shoved the hard drive in his bag and said, "Why don't you come to my office in the afternoon? I'll copy the data and you can take your hard drive."

"Sure, I'll let you know if I am coming down," I said.

I just wanted him to get out of my place and after he left, I went to Michael's restaurant to eat. I met Michael there but didn't tell him anything because he knew Shankar from a long time, and I had no idea how he would react if I told him anything. I thought it would be better to let him discover about Shankar's evil side on his own. I had my brunch and took a walk on the beach. I sat at the end of the beach and started smoking. Waves were splashing as if they wanted to get out of the sea. When I heard from my manager about my extended holiday, I was planning to take up some meditation crash course from Shankar, but now I didn't even know what he really was. I wished I hadn't met these people here in the first place. I should have been here all by myself and then it would have been less troublesome. What had happened couldn't be changed, but I was also feeling good that I came to know about Shankar before telling him anything. If this had happened after I told him everything, that would have been worse.

I smoked some more cigarettes till I started coughing my lungs out. After that I walked straight to my apartment. I had already started hating the place, not because of Shankar; I usually feel irritated if things around me don't seem alright. I took a bath and tried to sleep but ended up changing sides and restlessly crawling in the bed for I don't know how long, before I slept.

Next day, I woke up with a strong feeling that I didn't wanted to stay in Goa anymore. No doubt the place was good, but I didn't get anything concrete after coming here and if I decided to stay back any longer, I would end up wasting more time running behind sham things. Even before I brushed my teeth or ate something, I picked up everything and packed my luggage. I decided to go back to Bangalore and start everything from scratch. I could plan everything out on the way. I got ready and went down to the reception and told them that I would be checking out today. I went to the motorbike shop and returned the motorbike. Then I went to Michael's restaurant, I met him and told him that I would be leaving today because an important work had come up in office. Michael asked me if I needed any help. I asked for the total bill that I had to clear. I settled the bill and had breakfast there, and after that I called Shankar as I had to collect my hard drive from him.

"Can I come and collect the hard drive now? I am leaving today," I said.

"How come you are leaving today?"

"There's some emergency work at office."

"Oh! Then come to my office, I am here," he said.

I hoped there was something else I could have had as a last memory of this place. But the irony is that I was going to meet Shankar before leaving. I went to his office. He was sitting with a couple. They were foreigners and they had come to join his classes. He introduced me to them and asked me to sit there while he was talking to them. While I was sitting, there was no way I could escape his talks. He was talking about *chakras*, and he was telling them how to bring the power of *chakras* into practice, and how to activate our positive energy. The couple was listening to him carefully, but I was reading between the lines. I think he had mastered the art of conning people and he was good at playing with their weaknesses. He then started taking about the navel *chakra* and how to control the animal instincts and carnal desires. When he was talking about it, I thought even a chameleon wouldn't be able to match the pace in changing colour with this guy if it tries to. I wished these people could see his real face. But unfortunately they fell in his trap and looked very satisfied after listening to him. Who knows how many people he had fooled till now? But I was sure, hypocrisy didn't last long, and sooner or later he would be exposed. I was getting late as I wanted to leave Goa during the daytime. I tried interrupting but he didn't let me as he was busy with his conning spree.

Two-faced people like Shankar can be good at many things, but I think they should stop playing with godly words and the best they can do is not to hurt people with things which are considered to be spiritual and which has an effect on people's emotions. Shankar continued his talks for some more time and asked them to come and see him next day.

After all he did backstage, he still has the audacity to preach his talks with confidence. They took his brochure and left the place. Next was my turn. He went inside and brought my hard drive and gave it to me, and said, "Thanks for fixing my computer, Jackson. Did you see how interested those people were?"

"Oh yes, I did."

"It's sad to see our people are losing interest in tradition and foreigners are valuing our culture and getting benefit from it. Isn't this hypocrisy when we say we value our tradition and we don't practice it?"

The moment the word 'hypocrisy' came out of his mouth, I lost my control. I looked into his eyes and said,

"I saw what was in the hard-drive Shankar; don't play this being-saint card with me."

The moment I said that, he didn't even blink his eyes or move from his place for a few seconds. I got up and said, *"Goodbye!"* As I turned back, he got up and said, "Let me explain, what…," and then he started stuttering.

I was least bothered to listen to his justification and excuses and I walked out on him without looking back, it was like 'fool me once, shame on you, fool me twice, shame on me' scenario. Good thing was that I had packed my luggage earlier and all that was left to be done was to pay the apartment rent and get going. I cleared the bill and dumped my luggage into the car and left. On the way, I stopped at Michael's restaurant to bid him goodbye.

"Inform me at least a week before you come next time," he said.

Michael was good to me all the time and was very helpful as always treated me as a friend.

8

Back in the Belly of Beast

I hit the road and I was back to square one again. I was ready to go back into the belly of the beast. Though I was headed to Bangalore, I still had a mixed feeling whether to go home or not. Though my final destination was home, I still had an inclination to take a different route. I didn't take the usual route from which I came. I thought of taking a new route even if it was longer. I drove around 80 kms from Goa and stopped at a place to have coconut water because what could be more refreshing than coconut water under the hot burning sun. I had three of them, one after the other. I was standing right under the tree for some fresh air. While I was having the drink, a car came by and stopped near me. The car had Bangalore's registration. Four guys got down from the car to have coconut water. One of them came up to me and asked for a lighter. He lit the cigarette and asked me, "Are you coming from Goa?"

"Yes."

"How was it? I mean the crowd?"

"It was good," I said.

"Oh thank God, we are coming from this place called Gokarna. God, it's the most unhappening place we have ever been. We couldn't stay there more than a day. We are off to Goa now."

"Why? What happened?" I asked.

"That place was so boring and even the beaches are empty. You'll hardly see people around."

Empty beaches and no crowd, what more did I need? I saw a potential opportunity in what he said. It sounded like a perfect place to practice my isolation. "How far is this place from here?" I asked.

"It may be 60-70 kms ride from here. And it's on the way to Bangalore," he said.

As it came on the way, I thought of stopping by and checking out the place. The road was narrow and curvy all the way and the climate was hot as hell. Whenever there was a straight road, there was a mirage waiting to deceive. I remember from a movie where there were a group of people crossing the desert and they ran for water desperately whenever they saw a mirage, and finally they saw a mirage where birds were flying on the top and that's when they realised that it was not a mirage, as birds won't get deceived by mirages. I think there are things meant to deceive certain things.

As they said, it was around 70 kms from there, I entered the town. It was a typical coastal area of Karnataka. Everything was written in Kannada, from flex boards on shops to the posters on walls. I couldn't read Kannada so well but I spoke the language pretty well. I spoke to people to get the directions, and their accent was different from what people speak in Bangalore. Still, it was manageable for me as they understood what I was speaking.

I stopped at a small restaurant to get an idea about the place. I spoke to the restaurant owner and he informed that there were four to five beaches in Gokarna and out of them, there are only two main beaches where they have beach shacks to stay. I spoke to a couple of other people to inquire about the place after which I discovered that the most popular beach was the Om beach, which was 10 kms away from the town. They showed me the route and I had to climb the hill and then get down for next 5 kms. The road was curvier and only one vehicle could pass at a time; if another vehicle came from the opposite direction, either of the two vehicles had to give way.

This place was entirely different from Goa and I had to climb down the stairs to get to the beach. While getting down, something struck my mind and I froze and saw the beach. I felt like I had been to this place before. It was like a *Deja vu*. Earlier I used to get fascinated whenever I used to have any such experience. But these days everything was jumbled in my life, and I wasn't able to figure out what was real and what was virtual. I came down and walked across the beach, and as I had heard, it was quite empty; in fact, far more empty as compared to Goa. I liked the beach the very moment I stepped on it. I walked till the other end barefoot. I saw around 10 shacks along the beach. I went to a shack which was at the end of the beach and asked them if they had any space to rent, but unfortunately all were occupied.

"Is this the season time?" I asked.

"No sir, the season is coming to an end," the man said.

I thought of eating something there and ordered my lunch. After finishing the lunch, I went to a few other shacks to check. But all of them were full as well. I lost the hope of getting any shack on that beach. I came back and asked a few auto-rickshaw drivers about the shacks. They suggested me to try in Kudli beach which was close-by. They also informed me that I can't take my car there because the road was messed up. So, I took an auto-rickshaw and went to Kudli beach. Like they said, the road was in shambles up pretty badly, and there was no way I could have made it in the car. Again I had to climb down from the muddy hill to get to the beach. This beach was smaller when compared to Om beach; I was hoping to get a shack here. Similar to Om beach, there were shacks with restaurants attached to them. I went inside a restaurant and asked for a shack, but the restaurant owner turned me down by nodding his head. After me, a foreigner walked in and asked for a shack and the owner said, "Yes sir, we have it." I was shocked to hear that and I asked him in Kannada, "Right now, you just said no to me?"

"Please give way, sir," he said.

I stepped aside and that foreigner filled the register and got inside. After he left, I asked the same question to that guy. He lied on my face, "He had a prior reservation, sir!"

As if I was dumb and did not understand English. I was tired and wasn't in a mood to fight with him. I left the place and checked in five more shacks and all of them said 'no' without any reason. I couldn't figure out the reason behind the denial. I climbed that hill and came out. No doubt I was angry with these people, but I really liked the place, especially the Om beach and I didn't want to leave so early. Anyway, I had two more weeks off and I thought of renting a room in a hotel back in town. I took an auto-rickshaw back to Om beach, where I had parked my car. On the way, I asked the auto-rickshaw driver, "Why are they not renting the shacks?"

"They prefer foreigners, sir," he said.

"What do mean by 'they prefer foreigners'?"

"That's the only income we have here sir and if we accommodate them well, they'll come back the next season."

That was logical but they should think of localities too. I reached Om beach and took my car from there and drove back to the town. I found a hotel where they had a good parking facility. I booked a room, dumped my luggage and took a cold water bath, which turned out to be very refreshing in that humid weather. After that, I came down to the reception to ask more about the place. There was a receptionist named Suresh who was a young boy who got excited whenever anyone queried him about the place.

"This is primarily famous for the temples sir; we have ancient temples here."

"Where are these temples?" I asked.

"It's close by sir. It's walking distance from here," he said.

It was evening by now I thought of going to the beach in the morning; hence I made up my mind to visit those temples. I took directions from Suresh and left for the temple. On the road, I saw the old houses which had wooden poles outside, with corridors. Old men were sitting outside, staring at people who passed by. There was no traffic or hooting noise. The streets were empty and most of the people who were walking by looked cheerful. I kept asking for directions and finally made it to the temple. It was dark by the time I reached there and there was no way I could see everything in that darkness. After all, I wasn't in a hurry; I had all the time in the world to explore things. On my way back to the hotel, I saw a few south Indian restaurants. It had been a long time since I had tasty food. I rushed into a restaurant and ate an amazing meal after ages.

There was a tilted wooden bench right outside the restaurant. I sat on it, stretched my legs and took a deep breath. It was simply refreshing. Due to the cold breeze and empty street, I just closed my eyes and started breathing deeply. After a while I heard a bicycle ring and that broke my trance. I noticed an old man sitting next to me, wearing a white shirt and white *lungi* and smoking. He squinted at me, but didn't say a word. I took out my cigarette pack and asked him for a lighter. He took out a match-box from the pocket of his shirt and gave to me. I lit the cigarette and returned the match-box, saying, "It's a nice weather isn't it?"

"Oh yes, but it will be too hot during daytime."

"Oh, is it?" I asked.

"Yes, where are you from?"

"Bangalore," I said.

"What do you do there?"

I gave him a brief introduction. And before I could ask him something, he himself started telling about his life. I think I shouldn't have asked for a lighter. This old man narrated his whole life's saga. He told me about his hardships in early ages of life and how he slogged and worked to make money, and how he raised his children and how they abandoned him finally. Phew! What an irony, he told his story to someone who was in even a still worse condition than him. I think he wanted to unburden himself by telling this to someone. And yeah, like I said earlier, everyone considers their problems to be unique and bigger than others. I could perceive only one thing out of his sad story – there was no way I wanted to end up like him one day.

On the way back to the hotel, again my inseparable illness triggered. I was enjoying myself since the time I had reached there and when the night arrived, I came back to my old self. An unknown fear and sudden increase in heartbeat drove me crazy, and my jaws got locked. I felt like my head would explode. Nothing seemed to help me. Even after trying everything possible I ended up seeing the same scene over and over again.

I was sure that I wouldn't get sleep that night and was not ready to stay wide awake in bed for the whole night. I went to a chemist shop and asked for a tranquilliser. Luckily, I got a half strip of tranquilliser; there were four pills. The strip in my hand made me feel reassured. I knew it was all due to my mindset, but still I couldn't help myself. I took an auto-rickshaw from there and reached the hotel. I popped a pill and started feeling dizzy. I didn't realise when I fell asleep.

Next morning I woke up, feeling obliged towards the pharmacy guy who had given me pills without pestering me with questions regarding prescription. I got ready and came down, Suresh asked me about how the temple was. I told him that I couldn't go to the temple last night and I would be going there today. I was quite familiar with the roads by now and it didn't take me long to reach the temple.

I got inside the temple; it was old as I had heard. I circled the whole place and saw people chanting and praying; a few of them had books in their hands. After clicking a few pictures, I came out and made my way back to the beach. This time I wasn't looking for a place to stay; all I wanted was the cool and calm shade under a tree. Strangely this beach was covered with huge trees and there were less coconut trees around.

I sat under a tree, looking at the waves which were gushing towards the rocks and cleaned them with each flow. I had got addicted to the sound, I did not get bored, no matter for how long I heard them. After a while, I lay down using my bag as a pillow. A small kid came up to me. He was selling neck gears and other stuffs made out of stones. Till now this was the only common thing that I saw between Goa and this place.

I got up and left the Om beach. I wanted to see other beaches in Gokarna, so that I could spend more time on the beach which I liked the most. I hired an auto-rickshaw from there, and asked the driver to take me to all the beaches around. The auto-driver was a friendly chap. He took me to all the places patiently and in the end he dropped me at the hotel. After I got down from the auto-rickshaw, he asked me, "Why are you not staying at the beach, sir?"

"I went to a couple of beaches yesterday but none of the shacks had a vacant room."

"I know a place in Om beach, sir. I can take you there tomorrow if you want."

"Sure, I would love to see the place. Please help me with this."

I took his cell number and he said, he'll pick me up tomorrow morning from the hotel, and arrange a shack at the Om beach. I was pretty happy to know that I would get to stay on the beach. The next day I called the auto-rickshaw driver in the morning. I was with him for the whole day but I forgot to ask his name. Nevertheless, I called him, and he recognised my voice and said he'll come and pick me up. I also got his name; it was Ashok. I was waiting for him in the lobby, and he came within 15 minutes with a clean, shaved face and oiled hair.

We went to the Om beach; he took me to one of the places I had visited the first day when I reached here. Luckily, the owner of that place didn't recognize me. Ashok told him something while I was standing behind. After a while Ashok came up to me and said, "Sir, it'll be a little expensive."

"I am fine with that," I said.

I made the advance payment after which we went back to the hotel to check out. I left the car at the hotel as that was the only safe place available for parking in the town. I packed my luggage and finally I vacated the hotel and went to the beach.

9
Shack

There were six shacks on that beach and out of which, three were in a row. I was given a room which was at the right corner. It was made out of muddy walls and its roof was covered with tiles and coconut leaves. I didn't care much about the place; all I wanted was a beach to see when I got up in the morning. I had lunch at the shack; it was very comforting when I got everything on the beach. At the shack's restaurant, there was a small library which had books in French, German and other foreign languages. I kept flipping through them till evening, and went for a swim later. Swimming on an empty beach till the sunset was a sublime experience. I came back to the shack when it got dark. After freshening up, I came and sat in the restaurant, and ordered something to eat.

I finished eating and went to my shack to pop a pill that I had bought. I searched my luggage bags and everywhere around, I couldn't find the strip. I had lost my pills somewhere. It was impossible to get a new strip of pill at that time. There won't be any auto-rickshaw available, but still I called Ashok to check if he was available. To my disappointment, he wasn't around. I knew this was going to be another terrible night and I had to spend it all alone. I again opened my luggage and started searching. Meanwhile, a guy came at the door and said, "You need something pal?"

He was a foreigner. I guessed it from his accent.

"No, I am fine," I said.

The guy returned to his shack which was opposite to mine. I had a concerned neighbour here. I took my music player and went to the beach and sat there for some time. Every song I played led to boredom after a few minutes. There was a huge black rock, at the corner, I climbed on it and sat there, looking at the grim dark sea.

I sat there pitying myself with my thoughts; let me tell you, loneliness is the worst curse. After a while I broke down crying, I cried as loud as I could. I was missing Deepa and everything that I had. I wished she was here and I could tell her everything about the way I was feeling. I remembered those nights when I used to wake up in the middle of the night wondering where I was. And I would give her a call and she would tell me "Don't worry, I am here with you." Just her presence over the phone would give me the highest form of comfort. I wish I had someone to say, "I'm here, don't worry." But when I spoke to her the last time, she said she was a changed person now. I don't know what that meant and what had changed in her.

I remember one night, I had a severe chest pain and I was at the hospital all alone. I called Deepa and she came down immediately at 1 a.m. After I was treated, I slept on her lap, on a bench outside the hospital. She kept telling me stories until I felt better. Those were the moments worth recalling.

I sat on that rock for a long time, close to an hour. A little later, someone passed by with a torch in hand. That person flashed the light on me and walked away. I couldn't see who that was. I returned to the shack after crying my heart out. When I contemplated on the reason as to why did I cry so much, I could not come up with a logical reason and I laughed at my absurdity.

I was having trouble opening the lock in the dark and then the European guy saw me and asked, "You need a torch?"

"Oh yes," I said.

He flashed his torch on the lock and I opened the door.

Was he the one who had flashed the torch on me when I was sitting on that rock? I wasn't sure and I thought of asking him in the morning.

The next morning I woke up, disturbed by loud voices. There was a kind of a chaos in the restaurant at around 8 a.m. I came out and asked the people around as to what had happened and came to know that someone had drowned last night. I went to the beach and saw the police talking over their walkie-talkies. There were few fishermen walking around the place and I heard someone saying, "They took away the body early in the morning." I didn't bother to find out who was it. Death didn't amaze me anymore. When I saw people who were around, there was a particular fear on their faces. I knew what was running in their minds – it was *'I could be next'*.

I came back to the shack and saw the European guy who stayed in the opposite shack writing something in a small book. He looked at me and waved.

"Did you check what happened out there?" I asked.

"Oh yes, I did," he said and smiled.

I couldn't understand why he smiled!

"Pretty bad, isn't it?" I said.

"Oh yes, whoever has died must have realised something by now."

"What do mean?" I asked.

"Ah! Not much, people realise a few things, which they don't realise in their lives, after they die."

"Like what?" I asked.

"Like, this life was not created for nothing." He said that smilingly and then closed his little book and said, "Catch you later, mate," and went inside.

What did he just mean? Life was not created for nothing? What did he mean by that?

I had never seen anyone reacting in such a manner on hearing about some death news the way he did. He sounded like he knew exactly what had happened. I lit a cigarette and stood in the same place. He came out after a few minutes with his bag; probably he was going somewhere.

"I am sorry; I didn't get your name," I said.

"Hammy," he retorted and walked away.

After some time, I went up to the reception and started talking to the receptionist. His name was Chandu and he was pretty impressed after listening to my Kannada. My intention was to know something more about Hammy. After a while, I asked Chandu if I could check the register. He just handed over the register without cross questioning.

I flipped through a few pages, trying to check the names of the people who stayed over there. Hammy was staying here from one month and his full name was Hami Reza Clayworth. It sounded like 'Hammy' when he pronounced his name, may be because of the accent. He was from 'Bradford, UK'. Like I guessed by his accent, he was a British. But his name sounded somewhat weird to me.

Then I asked Chandu, "Why is this guy staying here from such a long time?"

He said, “Sir, people stay here for months and I don’t know why this guy is here and that too at the end of the season.”

“What is he like?” I asked.

“What do you mean, sir?”

“I mean, what does he do all time?”

“He stays up all night sir, and gets up by afternoon. I think he got up early today, may be because of what happened at the beach as there was so much of noise. His routine is the same every day.”

I gave the register back to him and had my breakfast. I couldn’t go out for some time as there were too many people at the beach, so I asked Chandu to play ‘blues’. I sat at the restaurant, enjoying the music for some time and after that I called Ashok as I wanted to go to the pharmacy store to get those tranquillisers. Ashok came down after an hour and I went to the town with him. I bought one more strip of pills and stocked it in order to assure sleep for the next 10 nights. While returning back to the beach, I saw Mr Hami going somewhere. I immediately asked Ashok to stop the auto-rickshaw. Hami looked at me and prompted a ‘Hi’.

“Where are you headed?” I asked.

“To the beach,” he said.

“Even I am going to the beach; let me drop you,” I said.

He paused for a moment and said, “Sure,” and he got inside.

I wanted to talk to him very badly and didn't know how to break the ice and start a conversation.

"What were you doing in the town?" I asked.

"I went to pick up the batteries for my torch," he said. And he asked me what I was doing there.

"I had been to the pharmacy," I said.

"Why, what happened?"

"I have this sleeping disorder, so I needed tranquillisers."

"Oh! That's bad. Are you taking any treatment for that?"

"Oh yes, I am taking treatment. I have insomnia from many years and it is creating even more problems for me these days."

He was sympathetic and we spoke on some general topic like the weather in India till we reached the beach. We got down from the rickshaw and started walking towards our shack. On the way, he said, "You should have a good diet and do some exercises along with your medical treatment. You know, it'll help you recover faster. And if you are doing some other bad stuff while you are taking a treatment, it'll mess everything up."

"I didn't get you?" I asked.

He smile and said, "I saw you smoking the other night on the rock."

Uh, I was right. It was him that night who flashed the torch on me.

"I was just smoking cigarettes," I said.

"Tobacco or marijuana, both can cause serious troubles my friend," he said.

Did he just call me a junkie? By the time I could reply back, we reached the shack and again he said, "Catch you later," and walked away. I was really pissed at the comment he made. He thought I was doping last night, but the case was totally different. He seemed like a sensible man but he turned out to be a judgmental ass, who presumed things without knowing the beginning or the end of the tale.

On that night I decided not to take any pills, even though I was feeling damn restless. People had started calling me a junkie because of my pill taking and smoking habits, and there was no way I could explain my state of helplessness to anybody. I spent that night staying up at the beach and I couldn't get sleep the next day as well, and at night. I was expecting sleep with some confidence as it was more than 24 hours I hadn't even winked. I waited till I realised that it was not going to be easy to get some sleep without taking the pill. Again, I spent one more sleepless night. People wouldn't have believed if I told them that I hadn't sleep since the past two days and two nights. This was not the first time this had happened, but it had happened after a long time. I saw Hami a couple of times but I chose to ignore him. I didn't feel like approaching him at all.

Let me tell you how it feels, after three days of sleeplessness, my backbone hurt badly. I couldn't sit straight at one place for more than 15 minutes and my eyes burned like hell, even when I closed them. The body was all tired and it gave up on me, but my mind stayed active with random thoughts. When I lay on the bed and tried to sleep, I stared at the roof or at the ceiling fan. I remember spending nights just by staring at the fan's screw and imagining how electricity passes though it and the whole mechanism of a ceiling fan.

After being awake for two days and two nights, on the third night I took a pill and slept for 17 or 18 hours at a stretch. I woke up in the afternoon, completely refreshed, as if I have been born again. I was starving to death. It was lunch time and the restaurant was full, but I managed to get a table.

10

A Mistake Again?

I was having my lunch when Hami came up to me with a glass of juice in his hand and asked, "Can I join you?"

"Sure," I said.

"How's it going? Your eyes are kind of swollen up."

"Yeah, I slept a lot," I replied.

Actually, I didn't know what exactly he was referring to.

"Oh you slept? How was it?"

"It was such a pleasure," I said.

"Pleasure!" after saying this he started smiling.

"Why, what happened?" I asked.

"*Naah,* nothing."

I didn't know what made him smile. Had I said something funny or did he derive something funny out of whatever I had just said? May be he thought I had some drugs before sleeping.

"I took sleeping pills before sleeping!" I said with sarcasm.

He was still smiling and said, "I am still thinking about what you said."

"What did I say?"

"You just said sleeping was a pleasure. I tried hard but I could never figure out which part of sleep can we take as a pleasure? I mean, when do we experience the pleasure while sleeping? Is it before sleeping or after that?"

That was a tricky question to answer; I thought for a while and said, "It is while you are sleeping."

"How could you enjoy that? You are already sleeping and you can't realise what's happening with you. Haven't you heard sleeping is half death?"

"In that case, I think it's before or after the sleep," I said.

"You are awake then? How can you get the pleasure of sleep?"

"So what's the answer?" I asked.

"There is no answer mate; it's just one of the delusional things of life."

"What do you mean by that?"

"Ah, nothing much."

He finished his juice by then and said, "I have to go, check my e-mails. Catch you later."

He went to the reception and gave something to Chandu and left the shack with his bag, torch and a smiling face. I wanted to stop him and ask something more on what he was saying, but I didn't know what stopped me. I was sure, he had something more to share on his end. I thought of catching up with him when he returned.

After that, I went for swimming and came back to the shack. Hami's words were running in my mind all the time. And out of desperation, I asked Chandu about his whereabouts. Chandu had no idea about it, and he said Hami may come back by 8 p.m. I sat in the restaurant, flipping through books and listening to the music. I waited till 9 p.m. I didn't even know if he would talk to me when he returned. I didn't feel like having dinner and went to the shack to watch a movie.

One more thing that I repeatedly did was watching a movie called '*The Shawshank Redemption*'. I might have watched it a zillion times, but still I can't get over it. I can relate my loneliness with the lead character in the movie; it pushes me towards the philosophy of hope. I have watched the movie so many times that even if it's played in a mute mode, I can deliver each and every dialogue of it. I watched '*The Shawshank Redemption*' till 1 a.m. and after that I was idle. I went out to check on Hami. I went to his shack and there was no one inside, but there was a night lamp which was switched on. Why would anybody switch on their night lamp and go? Or maybe he was back. I went to the reception but no one was around. When I stepped out of the restaurant, I saw Hami sitting right outside the gate, all alone. I can't explain how glad I was to see him there. I went up to him and before he could ask me anything, I said, "How come you are here?"

"I sit here every night buddy. You didn't get sleep again?" he asked.

"Oh I slept enough. How about you?"

"I don't have any specific time to sleep. I am not tried enough to sleep."

I sat next to him on the sand for a few minutes, without saying anything. We both were looking at the sea; it was dark and the waves were hitting the rocks. My curiosity to know Hami was at its peak, but my lack of ability to break the ice stopped me from asking anything. But, to my good luck, he himself asked, "I am sorry; I don't know your name yet."

"I am Jackson."

"So they call you Jack?"

"No, they call me Jako."

"Jako?"

"I don't know exactly. I think it started with my sister; she used to call me Jako when we were kids and after that my classmates picked it at school. I didn't realise when I got that name but it will be associated with me till I die."

He laughed and said, "That's good. You are different from other Jackson's then." He asked me more about what I did and other things about me.

After that, it was my turn to shoot questions. I knew his name already and I was curious to know about other things. I started by asking, "Where are you from? And what do you do?"

He said, "I am from England. You must have heard of Bradford. I used to be a professor in the university."

"You mean you are not working anymore?"

"Nah! I've had enough."

"What does that mean?"

"There comes a time in our life, when we have to get our 'ducks in a row'."

I couldn't make out what that idiom meant but it sounded like a sensible one. And then I said, "I can't believe you were a professor. You look pretty young to be a professor. What were you teaching? I mean what was your subject?"

He smiled and said, "I'm old enough to be a professor, mate. I used to teach philosophy; ever heard of epistemology?"

"No, what's that?"

"It's a branch of philosophy. I happened to do my Ph.D. in that topic."

That was completely an alien thing I had ever heard in my entire life. Can somebody study something like that? I wasn't aware of whatever he had said. I got more curious and asked, "Never heard of this; can you tell me more?"

"Hmm, I am sorry mate; it's a vast subject to talk on. But I'll tell you something which would give you an idea; you know what they call the 'fear of knowledge'?"

"No, I have no idea."

"It's called, *epistemophobia*."

"Uh, is this something to do with psychology?"

He smiled again and said, "Like I said, it's a vast topic."

I have heard British speaking in a heavy accent and especially people from England, but his accent was neutral and easily understandable.

"So you are born and brought up in England?" I asked.

"Oh yes, my Dad was Persian and my mother British."

"You know Persian too?"

He nodded his head and said, "Pretty well, my friend."

Oh God, I started imagining the vastness of the world which is filled with so many things which I had never imagined. I was sure that he won't go for any work at this time, so I asked him about what he had said during lunch, which had kept bothering me the whole day.

"I was thinking about what you said, Hami."

"About what?" he asked.

"About sleep not being a pleasure."

"Is it not?" he asked.

"I don't know. I was thinking about it but I couldn't understand the concept," I said.

"It's a pleasure or it's not a pleasure, I don't know that myself. It's a debatable topic without an answer. I could never reach a solution myself and it always makes me think, if pleasure is a state of mind, does it also require the presence of mind? Again it raises the question, when do we experience the pleasure? But I have convinced myself that it's an unsure pleasure which people consider as real pleasure."

When he said that, I became expectant that the conversation would go on for a long time. But all of a sudden, I started feeling dizzy.

"Not sleepy?" I asked him.

"You seem to be very concerned about sleep, aren't you?" he asked.

"Yeah, sleep is the best thing that can happen to an insomniac."

"Can I ask you something?" he said.

"Sure."

"Don't you think sleep should be in your control? And we should be above that?"

It seemed as if he was trying to help me in some way, but I don't know why. Suddenly Shankar's face came in my mind. "What if he is another Shankar?"I didn't reply to his question.

I smiled and said, "You are right, it should be in our control." I wanted to go back to the shack before he asked me something else. I got up, stretched my hands, yawned and said, "Isn't it too windy?"

"Oh yes, are you going to sleep?" he asked.

"Yes, catch you tomorrow."

I said this and walked back to the shack; I lay on the bed, thinking, '*What if he is another Shankar*?' Now I am convinced that everyone is not what they portray themselves to be and the worst part is, there is no way I can figure out what the reality of a person is. I wish I had some tool or some sort of an X-ray goggles which would enable me to see the real face. Anyway, if I was going to think about it the whole night, it would ruin my sleep. So I got up, opened my bag, took out the pill and popped it in my mouth and slept.

11
Confession

Next day, I woke up around 11 a.m. and came out of my shack. Since, Hami was my neighbour the first thing I used to see when I opened my door was his door, which usually remained locked most of the time.

From the time I reached here, all I had been doing was eating and taking pills. Whenever I thought of doing something new, some kind of an ill omen shadowed my efforts. I decided to do something new today; I lit a cigarette and took a walk along the restaurant's corridor. I saw Hami sitting on a chair with his legs stretched on the table before him. He was writing something in his dairy.

When I saw him, I gave a second thought. I thought I may be wrong in judging him or maybe I should talk to him for some time. Meanwhile I could interrogate him through normal conversation. I didn't know how I intended to do it, but I was sure I could make it happen. After all what could be more pathetic than Shankar?

I went near Hami's table and pulled a chair. He got disturbed and looked at me.

"Mr. Jackson," he called out excitingly.

"Can I join?" I asked.

"Oh yes, please."

Though I plotted so much in my mind to investigate his character, the moment he smiled and asked, "How's it going?"

I replied, "I would like to tell you one strange story."

He sat back straight and said, "Sure, what is it?"

"I was in Goa for a couple of days before coming here, and there was this person whom I met. And then, without beating around the bush, I told him everything about Shankar – his hypocrisy, how he tried to help me and how he got caught. He heard the entire story without moving and he hardly even blinked his eyes. After I finished, he closed his journal and took a deep breath.

"Interesting," he said.

"Haven't you met anyone like that before?" he asked.

"No."

"There is nothing to be upset about. When we can't find out the real nature of people, we end up falling into their apparent appearance; it's normal, don't worry.

The reason is, we see what people show us, and many a times we see what our mind shows us. Haven't you heard of a famous saying, '*When a thief sees a saint, all he sees are his pockets'?"*

"But how can they be such hypocrites and deceive people like that?" I asked.

"Because they know people are waiting to get fooled. You were lucky Jako that you happened to find out about him. There is no way we can perfectly or accurately find out what people have in their minds. Gone are those days where people used to do mind reading and other stuff. These days you just hack into someone's e-mail account; you'll get to know everything about them. I prefer to be a hacker than being a mind reader these days.'

This words made me laugh and I felt relieved for a while.

"I am going to the beach, would you like to join?" he asked.

"Sure, let's go," I said.

12

What is in It?

I picked up a glass of juice and took a walk with him. A little further to the right of our shack, there was a tree which was half buried under the sand, spreading its shade around. We went there and sat beneath it. Hami said, "Can I ask you something, Jako?"

"Yeah, sure."

"You don't seem-like someone who is interested in mediation and life-oriented aspects. Why would a guy like you end up looking for these things?"

"I am going through tough times of late and I am very disturbed and restless with everything which is happening around me. So I was looking for some sort of help. I didn't know that I would end up following someone like him."

"That's natural, Jako. We all end up seeking some sort of help when we go through tough times and it will be very difficult for us to determine what's right and wrong during those times. Worries and tensions block positive thinking; and on the other hand, the fact is, the world is full of blind imitators. People follow others for no reason. I am glad you found out what you had to find out. By the way, how did you reach here? Have you visited this place before?"

"No, it's the first time I am here, and what about you?"

"Same here, it's my first time too. I came to Mumbai for a seminar which lasted for three days, and after that, I went to Goa and then I came here."

"Oh you were in Goa? Did you like it?"

"Yes I liked it, but it was very crowded and I didn't get a peaceful place like this to sit on a beach. So I came here to isolate myself."

"How did you find out about this place?" I asked.

"I met a guy from Ireland in my hotel and he had visited Gokarna earlier and he suggested me to visit this place."

"So you like it here?" I asked.

"Very much. Even though I grew up on an island, I am still fond of beaches and the silence which surrounds them."

"What do you mean?" I asked.

"Have you ever noticed that when we look at the sea, we turn our backs to the world? No doubt there is so much to see on land but when we look at the sea, we shed all the materialism that we carry. What I mean is, we face the sea by turning our backs to the land."

Wow, that was an amazing thing which I had never realised.

"Are you into poetry by any chance?" I asked.

He laughed and said, "No buddy, I am just an ocean watcher."

Whatever or whoever he was, he seemed like a sensible man from every angle. He spoke as if he observes things clearly and keenly, as if nothing is blurred for him. No wonder this guy looked mysterious from the beginning.

I lit a cigarette and he wrote something in his journal and closed it.

"Can I ask you something, Jako?"

"Sure, what is it?"

"Imagine if Shankar was a genuine person without any faults, what would have you done?"

"Then I would have been with him and I may have taken up his courses."

"Till when?" he asked.

"Till the time I would have felt good and gotten rid of the problem that I am facing."

He smirked and said, "That's what I thought."

"What do you mean?" I asked.

"You wanted to reflect on your life and you wanted to think on matters which you had never thought of before, right?"

"Yes."

"So, these things were temporary for you. You would have got back to your normal activities after your recovery, right?"

"Yes, of course."

"Now tell me, isn't this hypocrisy on your part? That you became something for some time to get rid of your issues? You wanted to pretend like you were concerned about life and you have taken it seriously. But were you really concerned? It looks like you became something and you changed yourself for some time, just to dump your issues. I agree with you when you blame that person was indecent but did you ever think about this side of yours?"

I couldn't disagree with him when he brought this up. I felt like I was wearing a veil which he was removing slowly.

"You are absolutely right," I said.

And then I asked him, "What else could have I done? I was going through hell and I was very confused."

"Yes, I know how it feels during that phase. But, that's not a long-term solution. We should never use wise subjects as pain-killers."

"Then what do you suggest? I should have ignored what I saw and continued with that person?" I asked.

"No way. I didn't mean that. I am glad that you found out. There was no way that person could have guided you in the right direction; he himself needed help. You know why?"

"Why?"

"There is no way anybody can have knowledge and filth together in them."

"Why do you call it filth? Majority of people these days watch pornography," I said.

"It's simple, my friend. Ask anyone about their first experience with porn, ask them if they have felt guilty after watching it, and that very guilt is the answer. I don't know who has decided good deeds and bad deeds, but for me, anything which gives peace and happiness after I commit the act is a good deed and anything which makes me guilty and sad after I commit the act, is a bad deed. Isn't it simple? Imagine the feeling that you experience when you make a child smile and the experience when you slap a child. Most of the time the heart answers the questions."

"Now let me get back to what I was saying. There is no way these two can stay together. The reason is, the vessel should be clean before you pour something into it. Imagine someone has dirt in his/her mind and they want to acquire something pure. How can it possibly happen? I am not saying that they can't possess any knowledge, but I can assure you that it will not help them in any way. And what's the point of having something in you, which benefits others and destroys you?"

"That makes absolute sense, but how can anybody identify the real knowledge-keeper from the fake ones?"

"There is no way we can figure out what's the reality of any person because everyone wears a mask. Have you ever checked the meaning of the word 'person' in a dictionary'?"

"No," I said.

"It comes from a Latin word 'persona' which means 'mask'. There is a way I judge people and I find it very easy. For me, the real knowledge-keeper and the seeker of truth never seek for followers. He always seeks more perfection. It has to be the other way round. People should seek him. If you see someone who is marketing himself and seeking followers, he's still a seeker of followers. When will he become the seeker of truth? Let me tell you an old story which my Dad used to tell me.

"There was an old sage in a small town and people used to come and consult him on various things and they used to take his advice and opinion. One day a lady came to him with her six year-old son. After greeting the old sage, she complained to him about her son. She said her son ate a lot of sweets and in spite of all possible effort, she couldn't stop her son from eating sweets. She asked the sage to talk to her son and ask him to stop eating sweets. The sage heard the whole story and asked the lady to come after a week. The lady couldn't understand the reason and she didn't argue with the sage but left the place quietly. After a week, she again came to visit the sage with her son. This time, the sage spoke to her son and said; 'Son, please don't eat sweets; it's not good for your health'. This instance surprised the lady and she spoke out this time, 'Master, I thought you will give him some medicine this time, but you just spoke to him. Why didn't you do it the last time when I came?' The sage smiled and said, 'I myself used to eat lots of sweets every day. How can I ask someone to stop something which I myself do? From past one week, I haven't eaten any sweets so now I am fit to advice your son'."

"Oh God, you are one hell of a professor," I said.

"Oh yes, I may be one," he winked.

After we spoke informally without any inhibitions, I thought we could continue like this. Meanwhile I started feeling quite comfortable with him and I knew that I won't be at any loss if I share my personal problems with him. But the problem was, I didn't know for how long he was going to stay here. Out of curiosity I asked him, "How long are you planning to stay here?"

"I may leave any time soon, mate; may be next week. What about you?" he asked.

I could afford to stay for one more week, and above all I didn't want to miss his company, so I said, "Even I am staying here for one more week."

"Are you on a vacation, Jako?"

"Not exactly, I didn't plan this. I just happened to take a break from my work."

"That's wonderful; we all need a break. Isn't it?"

"Yes, I think I deserved one," I said.

"Why did you come to this silent and calm beach? Shouldn't you be looking for some happening place?" he asked.

"Yeah I wanted to, but after coming here I realised that I had always wanted to come here."

"What do you mean by that?" he asked.

"You know it felt like a *Deja vu* when I first saw this place. So I think I had to come here. I was meant to be."

"Oh interesting, you follow *Deja vus*?" he asked.

"Yes, sometimes I do. I have seen this beach in my dreams before; may be this was my future that I had to experience."

"How serious are you with *Deja vus*?" he asked.

"It depends; I think it happens for a reason and they have a message to convey," I said.

He smiled over it and said, "Every accident is not our fate pal. Yes, I agree that *Deja vus* have a reason. But you can't say every *Deja vu* has a good reason, few *Deja vus* can occur as warnings too. If every *Deja vu* happens for a good reason, where has our free will gone?

"Free will? Does something like that exists in the world? I don't think there is any free will, sir. Everything has been decided and we are just walking through it," I said.

"You really think that?" he asked.

"Absolutely!"

He picked up a stone and said, "If that's true, can I throw this stone into the water?" he asked.

"If it's in your fate, you'll do it, and if it's not, you can't," I said.

"Then let me create my own fate. I'll bury this under the sand." He buried a stone under the sand and covered it. And then he said, "See, I just created my own fate or I just changed it."

"What do you mean? How can we possibly change anything? We can't change our fate, right?"

"I would have agreed with you completely if there was no free will," he said.

"Free will? If I had that, I would have been somewhere else, living happily. Even though I don't believe in God, I have faith in fate."

"I thought you were here of your own will, pal."

"May be or maybe not. May be I am living my fate right now."

"What if I tell you it's a combination of both?"

"I didn't get you. How can it be both?" I asked.

"What I mean is, fate and free will go together. Imagine, there are two cups on the table. One has juice in it and another has alcohol. Now, you have the free will to choose one of them. After you choose anyone out of them, it becomes a part of your fate.

"There was a wise person and someone asked him the difference between free will and destiny or decree, and immediately the wise man asked the questioner to lift his one leg. The man lifted his one leg and stood on the other one. The wise man asked him to lift his other leg as well.

"The man got confused and asked, 'How can I lift the other leg as well?'

"The wise man said, 'The first leg that you lifted was your free will and the other one is destiny.'

"If it's that simple and logical, why do you consider fate and believe in it?"

"Because there are things which are not under our control."

"Like what?" I asked.

"The time we are born in, our parents, our gender, etc. didn't exist. Maybe I would have been on your side."

"So, you mean that there is someone somewhere, controlling and deciding things for us, right?"

"I am not certain about that Jako, but yes there is something which keeps the cycle of things running appropriately."

"I think there is one more thing that we can choose on our own."

"What's that?" he asked.

"Our names."

He burst out laughing and said, "But now we have an option to change it. Isn't it good?"

"Yeah, I wish there was some way to go back in time or in future."

"Yes, I wish that too," he said.

"How about lunch?" he asked.

I immediately checked the time and it was 3 p.m. "Oh yes, it's lunch time," I said.

We got up, stretched our legs and folded the bedspread and started walking towards our shack. I was thinking how time flew by. I didn't even realise it was 3 p.m. and I wasn't even hungry. I didn't even bother to check the time while I was talking to him. I don't know whether my

Deja vu had a good meaning or bad, but I just felt pleasant being here and meeting him. Was he in my fate? Or it's just a coincidence that I met him. Whatever it was, I would surely think about it later. Right now, he's around me and that's what matters.

We reached the restaurant and Chandu looked at us awkwardly, may be he was shocked to see us together. We sat on the table facing the sea and yes I was also hungry by that time.

Chandu gave us the menu, looked at me and said, "Making new friends, sir?"

I smiled back and didn't say anything. Hami didn't understand what Chandu had said as he spoke to me in the local dialect. I started going through the menu and Hami placed an order immediately. He took vegetable salad for lunch. Even I wanted to try what he ordered but I was too hungry to experiment. I thought what if it turns out to be bad? Then I ordered my usual, heavy, Indian meal. Hami was quiet for some time. Then he opened his journal and closed it. Now, I had learnt to break the ice and so I easily started the conversation with him again.

"Don't you take pictures?" I asked.

"Naah, I don't like photography, Makes me feel too virtual. Oh I am sorry! "Do you like photography?" he asked.

"No, I am very bad at photography."

"That's a good reason," he laughed.

Chandu brought lunch for both of us together and we started eating. Hami wiped his spoon and fork with the tissue paper and started picking the carrot pieces.

"Hami, I have a question for you," I said.

"Yeah what's that?"

"Given a chance to choose the period to be reborn again, which period will you choose?"

"Hmm, I will choose 13th century," he said.

"Why that?"

"That was a time where interesting people walked on this earth. I would have tried and met at least one of them."

I didn't know who was there in 13th century that he wanted to be with; I didn't ask him much.

"What about you? What period would you like to be born in?" he asked.

"Aah, I would like to be born in future, may be at least 100 years ahead. By the time I try to figure out how things work, I may just complete my life span. There won't be any room for boredom in life."

"Boredom?"

"Yeah boredom. Now, when I have everything that a man can desire and ask for, I have reached a point where boredom started bothering me more than anything. Whatever you have or whoever you have around, everything gets boring after a certain period. And I think boredom is also an incurable disease. Don't you agree?"

"Yes mate, I agree. But are you sure that everything gets boring?"

"Why will it not be?"

"You know, when I was your age, I always used to think about the things that makes human condition miserable. Even till date, I ponder on this, but so far I can think of only two things which can disturb human life."

"What are they?" I asked him anxiously.

"Poverty and ignorance," he said.

"Come on Hami, I was taking about the mental state and boredom. How are these two related to our conscience?"

"I know what you are talking about. Just imagine, when we don't have money, money becomes the main problem and when we have money, boredom becomes the problem. But on a bigger picture, I think poverty and ignorance are two aspects. Now let's consider your point. What do you think causes boredom?"

"When you have nothing to do or when you are tired of doing the same thing repeatedly," I replied.

"Now, don't you think doing something or having something that has an obvious end will bring you to the state of boredom?"

"Yes, but everything we have has an end to it."

"Relax, mate! Yes, everything has an end to it. We always desire something more from what we have and what we do. That's human nature and we can't change it. But the solution is that we have to know the reality of things that we know already. When we set high expectations from things without knowing their reality, and when they fail to meet our expectation, that's when we get bored and that leads to depression and the chain goes on.

And at the root of it is our ignorance. The way I describe ignorance is different from what others perceive it. For me, ignorance is not knowing the reality of something, but of 'lacking knowledge'."

"Did you get it?" he asked smilingly.

"Not clear yet," I said.

"Okay, let me explain. The cure for boredom is thoughts; not just the thoughts but the constructive thoughts. You were right when you said boredom is a mental state. But the mistake we do is we always do physical activities to get rid of boredom. We go partying, we go out and play, we travel, etc. I am not saying that these are bad, but they are not the long-term solution because boredom affects our mind, not our body. If body is in trouble, I would suggest all the above techniques. But here we are dealing with our mental states."

"So what do you think I should do when I get bored?" I asked.

"Think something intellectually and if you can't, read something which attracts your intelligence. And yes, read only when you run out of thoughts and stay away from the ignorant. Isolation and loneliness are better than the company of the ignorant."

"How can anybody spot the ignorant?" I asked.

"It's simple, when know are their traits. An ignorant is the one who hurts you when you accompany him and insults you when you leave him. He will trap you with his favours if he gives you something, and will show ingratitude if you give him something. He will certainly betray you if you share your secret. He becomes ungrateful and arrogant if he's rich, and he will blame God when he is poor. He exceeds his limits when he's happy, and gives up when he's sad. He will praise you excessively if you please him, and he will withdraw the praise if you don't."

"This is like a tool to judge people. And what's with poverty?" I asked.

"That's the worst thing that can happen to the human race. Poverty will break you to such an extent that you can't even think for yourself, forget about being moral or immoral. You can't talk anything about a poor man until you change his condition. It's like a hungry man won't understand anything until you feed him.

"Did you get it now?" he asked.

"Yes, I did. I think, I should join your school now," I smiled.

When we finished our lunch, Hami decided to go and take a nap. He said he would meet me later. After that, even I thought of getting some sleep. You wouldn't believe if I tell you that I slept that afternoon and why wouldn't I sleep? After all, I had passed such an awesome day with Hami and I was able to shed all my mental worries. No wonder they say, happiness is a real comfort.

13

A New Beginning

I wanted to take a small nap but I ended up sleeping for almost six hours. I woke up because of suffocation as there was power cut and the fan wasn't working. I got up and checked the time thrice just to make sure that I had slept for so long. It was around 11 p.m. and I was hoping that Hami was awake. I took a bath and went to the restaurant. There I saw Hami playing Ludo with Chandu and the other boys. Usually after 10 p.m., you won't find anyone outside their shacks except the late sleepers or the crazy heads.

I went up to Hami and said, "Hey! How's it going?"

He turned back and said, "I am doing great; how about you?"

He always got excited when he met people and that made them feel like they were important to him.

"I am planning to go and sit at the same place where we were in the morning. Would you like to join me?" he asked.

"Sure I will." Honestly, why wouldn't I?

Hami said he'll wait for me in his shack. I finished my dinner. Thanks to Chandu, he prepared food anytime I asked him to. After that, I went to my shack and picked up the bedspread. I usually took the bedspread, which Chandu gave me as an extra when I checked in. Somehow I managed to take it to the beach without Chandu noticing it. I grabbed that bedspread and stuffed it into my bag and knocked on Hami's door. He was all set for a night out at the beach. As I mentioned earlier, he always carried his torch with him.

We both went to the same place where we sat in the morning; the credit went to Hami's torch. The place looked a little scarier in the night, especially the half-buried tree. We spread the bedspread and sat on it as if we were descending on our throne. After a while, Hami asked, "Would you excuse me for few minutes?"

"Sure," I said.

Hami got up from the place where he was seated and walked a little further towards the beach and sat in a position which looked like he was meditating. After a few minutes, he said something aloud and then immediately opened his journal and wrote something. I couldn't hear what he said. So I got up, went to him, and asked, "What happened?"

He smiled and looked up at the full moon and said, "I just turned 38, my friend."

"Oh, happy birthday!" Then he got up and I shook his hand and gave him a hug.

"This calls for a party," I said.

"Sure, what do you want on this beach?"

"Why didn't you tell me earlier? I would have arranged something at the restaurant or we would have planned something else."

"That's so kind of you, mate. I wanted it to be simple."

I was happy to know that he took me along and didn't hide his birthday from me.

"What did you say aloud?" I asked him.

"I said, 'Nothing has changed me.' When I look back on my past and my current state now, I see no difference and I want to rejoice about the fact."

"That's wonderful. How about going back to the restaurant and I can ask Chandu to arrange for a bottle of whisky? What do you say?"

"Ah! I don't drink, mate."

"What?"

"Yeah, I never did."

"You must be kidding me."

"I swear I don't."

"Why is that? Is it a religious obligation?"

"Absolutely not."

"I can't believe you have never tried alcohol. Why is it?"

"You know, what is the only thing that separates a human from animals?"

"What?"

"Our consciousness and if there is something which takes away your consciousness after consuming it, why would you want to try that?"

That was the best rebuttal I had ever heard in my entire life.

"But how do you know that it affects your consciousness? You never even tried it," I asked.

He smiled and said, "Most of the time we have to learn from others' mistakes. We never touch the fire to know if it's hot or not."

I was numb after hearing that and I couldn't agree more.

"What about the religion then? Are you an atheist?" I asked.

"No, I am not an atheist. I could not find any proof that there is no God."

"So, you do believe in God?"

"I believe that there exists an absolute power which I can't comprehend by any means."

"So you don't follow any religion?"

"Pal, first I need to know myself and then I can follow or believe in something. Let me ask you this, Can God create another God'?"

"What kind of a question is this?" I said.

"I am just entertaining a possible doubt."

"No, God cannot create another God," I said.

"That means you are limiting God. So, God is incapable of creating another God?"

"No, I didn't mean that. I think he can create another God."

"So, there are two gods now? Should I worship the first one or the second one?"

I didn't know what to say and I kept quiet.

"You want an answer?" he asked.

"Of course, I need an answer," I said.

"The answer lies in the definition of God. Every religion considers God as the Creator. So whatever is created cannot be a God. So, yes! God can create another God, but one that gets created cannot be considered God because it contradicts the definition of God."

"I have one question for you Hami."

"Shoot," he said.

"If God has a prior knowledge of where I am going to end up, why doesn't he just gives me heaven or hell? Why did he put me through so many problems?"

"You have asked me an open-ended question, Jako. I will certainly reply to this if you answer one small question which I have."

"You have a question for me?"

"Don't worry, it's very simple."

"Sure, then ask."

"What do you think life is? Answer me in one word, if possible."

I thought for a while, actually I pondered over my past and said, "Test!"

"Brilliant, that's exactly what I thought you would say. When life is a test, what do think makes the test fair and valid?

"I don't know," I said.

"Let me explain. It's the difficultly and the challenging aspects of the test which make it valid and fair. The more difficult the test is, the more value it has. Do you think an easy test will have any value? Imagine a student who is attending his important exam and that turns out to be a piece of cake, when it was supposed to be a difficult one. Don't you think that will turn out to be a joke?

"And actually, wise people, who are serious about their lives, always appreciate tests and they will handle them wisely, and they will never complain on being tested.

"What if a student in the middle of the exam complains to the professor that the exam is tough and it requires efforts and intelligence? The professors may reply that's the whole purpose of your coming here to take up this exam. Similarly, if we acknowledge that we are here to pass through the test of life and that's our whole purpose, we will never complain."

"And what about knowing ourselves mean?" I asked.

"To begin with, start figuring out your limits. Isolate yourself and think on the things which you cannot do. For example, you can't fly, you can't be in two places at the same time, etc. Are you getting what I am trying to say?"

"Yes, I am getting it."

"The reason is, our mind is limited and we have installed so much of unnecessary data in it. There is so much that we have to unlearn. The moment the unwanted data gets erased, you can fill what is required and important. And trust me, you can't keep the mind empty. It gets filled with or without your permission; all you need to do is filter it."

Hami made more sense when he was silent. When he finished his talk and the silence that he acquired after that was more interesting. I don't know what made him the way he was.

"Okay and how about your birthday celebration now?" I asked.

"Ah! Let's do something tomorrow," he said.

"Like what?"

"We can visit the jungle tomorrow."

"Jungle?"

"Yeah jungle. You know when I reached here a few weeks back, I tried to walk from this beach to another, and on the way I explored a little and found a small hill. We can camp there if you like. I have a tent. We can put up there.

"Sure, why not? How far is it?" I asked.

"Two to three miles from here," he said.

"That sounds pretty far," I said.

"It's just two to three miles. We can walk easily."

"Not for a smoker whose stamina is very low."

"Don't worry, we can take breaks."

"Yeah, I will need frequent breaks."

"You seem to give up before getting started, don't you?" he said.

"I still can't believe that you don't drink," I said.

"Yeah, believe it or not, I never even took a sip of alcohol, but I had an alcoholic woman though."

"You had?"

"Yes, we are divorced now."

"Why, what happened? Oh, I am sorry it's none of my business," I said.

"That's fine; she was looking for a husband and I was looking for a copassenger; she wanted a partner and I wanted a company. And honestly who wants to be with a wandering soul? May be, we weren't meant to be together," he said as if he enjoyed it.

If Hami was a girl, I would have fallen on her feet and proposed to her, no matter how old she was or where she was from. Sometimes people lose the best that they get.

"So you miss her now?" I asked.

"Yes I do," he said.

"Nothing is permanent, right?"

"Yes, nothing is permanent; we have to make it last," he said.

"How is that possible? Everything goes away sooner or later."

"That's exactly the answer; we have to let things go if we want them to remain with us. Once we sacrifice them, they'll make such a place within us that we won't be deprived of them anymore. But the sacrifice has to be from your own will; without any influence from outside. Try doing this at least once in your life."

When he said that, I was regretting not doing this with Deepa when I sensed her true intentions. What a fool I was that I allowed her to play with my emotions.

"So you let her go?" I asked.

"Yes, that's exactly what I did."

"When did this happen?"

"Almost 16 months back," he said.

"And how are you dealing with your loneliness after that?" I asked.

"It's amazing. Loneliness and isolation come with the potential opportunity and I enjoy every moment of loneliness by exploring myself. See, I am sitting here on this calm beach under the full moon on my birthday."

"But don't you miss people around? Don't you feel that you need someone to share your thoughts and feelings?"

"That's the mistake we commit. We expect people to be there and listen to us. Like I said before, expectation is the cause of depression and loneliness and it can drive a man insane."

"You know you should become a guru here. I am not joking Hami, you will do a better job," I said.

He smiled and said, "I don't want to make a living out of what I know. I prefer doing something which I am not good at for a living. If you are good at something, I think you should keep it to yourself."

"And by the way, what do you keep writing in that journal of yours?" I asked.

"It's something that I write for myself," he said.

"Can I have a look at it?"

"Sure," and he gave it to me. I turned the pages till the end, and it was almost full. The whole journal was handwritten and though I had a torch, I couldn't read anything clearly from it. I gave the journal back to him and told him that I'll check it some other time.

Towards our left hand side, a little far from where we were sitting, we saw a fireball circling. There were a few people sitting around the camp fire next to it. Since the time I came here, it was the first time I had seen something like that. I asked Hami if he had seen something like that before, and he said 'No'!

We got curious and took our belongings and started walking. As we were getting closer, we could hear somebody playing the guitar. When we reached the place, there was a group of foreigners playing the guitar and frame drum, sitting around the fire.

As usual, Hami said 'Hey' loudly and they replied to him in a same tone. "Can we join you?" Hami asked. They welcomed it and made a place for us to sit. What we saw from far was this guy playing with fire. He was doing all possible fire tricks. He was blowing fuel from his mouth to the fire, and he had a rope, which had fire at its end. He was spinning it in all possible ways. I wanted to get up and make an announcement that it was Hami's birthday today, but Hami didn't wanted to reveal it.

So I censured my act. I am sure he was enjoying the old school country music those guys were playing. Even I kind of liked that music, may be because it was live and the atmosphere was perfect for it. After a while, the fire player stopped his show and left the place. People, who were sitting around, started to vacate the place one by one and even the firewood turned into ashes. The only ones left were the insomniacs. I wasn't sure in which category did Hami fall?

I checked the time and it was 3 a.m. Since we had planned to camp the next day, I told Hami that I'll go and sleep because there was no way I could be active tomorrow if I didn't close my eyes for a few hours. I told him happy birthday once again and came back to my shack. Hami was sitting on the beach all alone; I didn't know what was running in his mind. If I would have asked him something, he may have replied which would have been beyond my comprehension.

Next morning, I went to the town to check my e-mails. I tried calling Ashok but he didn't answer my call. Nor did I see him anywhere near the parking area outside the beach. There was a carnival that was going on in the town. People had their faces painted and they were dressed in colourful clothes. When I asked about it, they told me it was some local festival.

I checked my e-mails. There was no update from my office. I thought of calling my manager and asking him if there were any updates, but then I thought it to be a bad idea. What if he asked me to get back? And on the other hand, I saw seven to eight text messages from my Dad. All had the same message. *'How are you doing? Call back.'* I called my Dad and apparently my mother was back from US, so I ended up speaking to both of them. They asked me to get back soon, if possible. I gave them an assurance that I would come back soon. But here, my stay depended upon Hami's stay. I got back to the shack. Hami was playing with dogs. Each time I saw him, I got these positive vibes. How can anybody be so content with life, even after going through so much? He looked at me and said, "Are you ready to nail the tent?"

"Aye, aye Captain! Lets sail," I smirked.

"So where were you?" he asked.

"I had been to the town. Went to check the e-mails."

"Oh, you should have taken me along. Even I wanted to use the Internet."

"I'll keep you posted from next time," I said.

It was 12 at noon and Hami had already packed everything that was required for the camp. His tent had a separate bag dedicated for itself and there were other two loaded bagpacks with him. Chandu and the other guys at the restaurant were curious to know what was happening. At first, they thought Hami was leaving. Later, they thought it's something else. I think they asked Hami a million times as to what was he up to, and no matter how well he tried to explain, they didn't get it. Yes, the language problem. They must have had a hard time understanding his British accent. Anyway, I explained to Chandu and others about our plan and I told them we will return in a day. We finished our lunch by 1 p.m. and I just took one small bag with some clothes as I was sure that Hami had packed the rest.

We left our shack at around 1:30 in the afternoon. I was carrying one water container and I had one bagpack. Hami had one water container and two bags. We started walking when the bright sun was still on our heads. The real problem was climbing those broken stairs to cross the beach and get to the road. With the heavy luggage which we carried, my lungs gave up on me. I felt breathless for a moment and I made Hami take our first break as soon as we reached the top. Even he was tired and we deserved a breather.

"Don't worry there are no more stairs after this," he said.

I couldn't even tell Hami that it was the wrong time to walk, because we needed time to set up the tent. We walked around 4 kms straight towards the town and then we took a right turn. There was no concrete road to the place we wanted to go. Wherever we saw a plain empty place without bushes, we walked on that and Hami remembered the route perfectly. We walked another 3 to 4 kms after taking that right turn.

Hami pointed towards a mud hill and said, "Jako we've reached!" It looked tiny from the distance he showed me, but when we got closer, it was bigger than I had assumed.

"Oh, it has a flat surface," I said.

"Yeah, that's exactly why I chose this place."

"What about this tent? You always carry this?"

"Nope, I carry this when I plan a long vacation," he said.

We unloaded our luggage there and sat for a moment. I lit a cigarette and asked Hami on how he was planning to make a tent.

"First we have to clean this ground," he said.

The ground was rocky and full of pebbles. "Let's get started then," I said.

"First we need to collect some firewood," he directed.

We looked around and there were plenty of dry sticks. We collected the sticks which were on the ground; we collected a decent amount of firewood. We made two bundles and kept them aside, and then we started picking up stones and pebbles to clear the ground for the tent. It was a pretty difficult work to do. And then, Hami took the tent out of his bag. It was just a piece of canvas cloth and I didn't understand how he was going to build a tent out of it. First he spread it on the floor and then he held its centre and pulled it upside. There was a rope in the middle which was outside the tent. He tied a knot to the rope. There was a tree at the corner, whose branches were stretched out. Hami threw the rope over a branch and pulled it to raise the central portion of the tent. And that gave me an idea that it was a workable idea. The tent wasn't in a triangle shape like I had imagined it to be, but it looked like a dome. Hami took out the hammer and the small rods. He nailed them to the four corners. After he did that, all the wrinkles disappeared and we had our perfect construction. Overall it took 30 minutes for him to build a tent and I didn't help him at all.

"So here it is," he said.

It looked perfectly amazing and the best part I liked about the tent was the door. It had two zips to it. I went inside and checked. It was ideal for two or three people to stay, but the surface was hard. When I told Hami about it, he gave me two bedspreads to spread it over the ground inside. I asked him if he had flicked it from the shack, he said he got it from Chandu.

"Is this safe here?" I asked.

"Just pray there are no wild animals here and I am not carrying any gun," he said.

That's the last thing to expect here and there was no way something of that sort could happen, because no animals can survive in a barren place or the heat. By 5 p.m., we had our tent ready. Oh I forgot to mention the real thrilling part. From the mud hill, we could clearly see the beach. I wasn't sure if we could see anything at night, but the view was clear in the evening.

Hami had separated the thick sticks from the broken ones in the bundles. And he had half a bottle of fuel to light the fire. By then, we had completed everything. Of course, my contribution was less and the man of the show was Hami. Hami had four bottles of orange juice. We both sat outside the tent and started sipping the orange juice, looking at the beach from the distance.

"So, how is it?" Hami asked.

"This wouldn't have been possible without you," I said.

"Never done camping before?"

"No," I said.

"Was this the part of your *Deja vu* by any chance?" he asked and laughed.

I don't know yet, maybe I should wait for some more time and something may trigger.

"I hope it turns out to be good," he said. And then he took out his journal and pen from his bag. That was the only thing missing to complete his presence. I wanted to check his journal this time; since it was still evening, I could read it.

14

An Ocean without Shore

"Can I see your book?" I asked.

He paused, looked at me for a moment and said, "Sure."

I started turning the pages and trust me, though it was written in English, I could hardly read any of it. I guess it was in old English, where they write 'where art thou' instead of 'where are you'. Now his journal was not of any use to me. Before closing it, I saw a poem on the first page of his book. It was…

Oh beloved,
Take away what I want.

Take away what I do.
Take away what I need.
Take away everything,
That takes me away from you.

I read these lines and looked at the sea. It blew my mind so quickly that I didn't realise where I had travelled and returned in a moment.

"You wrote this?" I asked.

"Which one?"

I showed him the first page.

"No, that's not mine; it's the translation of an Old Persian poem.

"Did you like it?" he asked.

"I loved it."

"Did somebody write it for the loved one?"

"I don't think so; some mystic wrote that and may be he's referring to God."

"It's so wonderful Hami, may be the best poem I've ever read."

"Oh there are plenty like those," he said.

"Is it? Where can I get them?"

"Relax, I will tell you. But I didn't expect these things would catch your attention."

"What are you saying? Why can't it be? It's so beautiful and who doesn't like beauty?" I said.

"That's true, but I fell for the poet, not for the poem," he said.

"What do you mean?"

"Imagine how beautiful he must be that his thoughts are like this. When he can write this, he can also write many like these."

"Yeah that's true. But we always tend to fall for what we see, right? Even with the beauty."

"Yes, it's a good thing to have something beautiful around you as it makes you feel good, and it's a natural human tendency. But I always think what someone might have done to itself to be that beautiful?"

"Sorry, I didn't get you."

"Imagine when you see a beautiful woman or an adorable baby, wouldn't you get attracted towards it?"

"Yes, it's natural like you said."

"Now tell me, what has that baby done to itself to be that adorable?"

"Nothing," I said.

"Exactly, nothing! Credit should go to the parents right?"

"Yes, you mean, we can't appreciate what we see?"

"I never meant that. I mean, we can praise people in two ways. First, is the way you described it. We praise what we see and I completely agree with that. But more praiseworthy is something which people acquire apart from what they are, like skills, knowledge, experience etc. In this case, the poem has done nothing to be praiseworthy by itself. All appreciation goes to the poet who imagined it in this way."

"It seems like I knew this, but I never thought about it this way."

"You like hearing all these, don't you?" he asked.

"Yes, only sensible things are making sense to me these days."

Hami pointed out to the beach and said, "Can you see that rock?"

"Yea I know, it's towards the left hand side of our shack," I said.

"I saw you sitting on it one night and I thought you were doing drugs."

"I wouldn't blame you for that," I said.

"What were you doing that night?"

"I was crying," I said.

"Crying? Oh! For what reason?"

"Ah it's a long and terrible story, man."

"I got all the time in the world, mate."

Seriously, I didn't know where to begin. Should I start with my recent worries or from the old ones? The truth is everything has the same impact. Hami was like an unknown priest who sat in the confession box of an unknown church. Telling him everything would be safe. I may not see him ever, after he leaves this place.

I started telling him my story from the beginning. I looked him in his eyes and said, "I had this restlessness right from my childhood days and I expected everyone whom I met to heal it. So I started figuring out things in my own way from my school days. As I grew older, I developed a strange loneliness, which is still not cured. I was always a lonely traveller in a caravan."

I said this much and paused for a moment. And then I continued my story and ended wish Deepa. I told him about how I spent my life, and how I wanted it to be. I told him almost about everyone whom I met in my life and what difference their presence made. I shared all my dreams and passions, and that I hadn't left my nightmares and troubles as well. I did tell him about who all I hated and who I loved, about my family and my job.

Finally, I concluded my story by saying; "I just couldn't take it anymore as the water had risen above the danger level and I thought of stopping and taking a break. That's how I ended up being here."

I swear, I kept talking for more than an hour and he didn't utter a word and heard me carefully. When I finished my tale, he got up and stretched his hands wide and said, "Interesting, mate, do you have an extra cigarette with you?"

"You smoke?"

"It's been ages. Can I have one?"

"Sure, I do," I gave him one cigarette.

He smoked a cigarette and we both were quiet for some time. I don't know what was running in his mind; he kept looking at the beach and when I checked the time, it was 7 p.m.

He pointed out to the firewood and said; "Can we light this?"

I got up and helped him pick the thick sticks and arrange it for the fire.

"Let's eat; we can light the fire after that," he said.

I was surprised for a moment as he wasn't talking about anything.

He had brought cereals and milk; somehow I managed to eat the cereals without sugar.

After we finished our formal dinner, Hami poured some kerosene on the sticks and lit the fire a little away from the tent on the flat ground. I offered him another cigarette but he denied it by saying, "I am good, thanks." I was hoping that he was not pissed off with me after listening to the story, because I was sure that there was something odd running in his mind. We sat down facing each other.

Hami suddenly smiled and asked me, "I didn't understand one thing."

"What?" I asked.

"So far you have never taken a step back and pondered over things. How did you do it this time? I am sure it's not because of your girlfriend or any other stuff. Did something happen to you? Did you experience anything?"

Now he forced me to tell him what I was hiding all this time. So, I told him the whole graveyard incident and how I buried that old lady. It was yet another confession for me.

After hearing this, he said, "Believe me, you have seen the glimpse of reality. What you went through has a profound significance. Let me tell you a secret. I am sure you may have never thought this way. I am telling this to you because you take the dream world seriously. And this may relieve you."

"Okay, what is it?" I asked.

"While we are dreaming, we consider our dreams to be our real world and we never realise that we are dreaming. But when we get up, we change our belief and claim that it was just a dream and this is the reality. In the same way, what if we realise some other reality after we die? It is possible, right?"

"Yes, we may," I said.

"So don't be so afraid of death because it's the most certain thing that will take place. Every soul shall taste death sooner or later. The best we can do is we can decide what matters and what doesn't in our lives; what to consider and what not to because we chase so many unwanted things constantly and we realise it when we are on our deathbed. Being remorseful on the deathbed would be too late. I mean, don't build your house on a bridge, because bridges are meant to be crossed. Let me tell you one small story.

"There was a sage who was walking in a remote place. On his way, he saw a beautiful girl whose beauty was very mesmerising. He stopped by and asked her what she was doing in such a remote place. She immediately replied to him, "I am a prostitute."

The sage smiled and asked her, "How many partners did you have?"

"I don't remember exactly, but every man who walked on this earth was my partner," she said.

"Were you loyal to them?"

"No, absolutely not. How can I be loyal? That doesn't suit my profession."

"Did they all love you?"

"Yes, they all did."

Then the sage said, "Fool he was who fell in love with you, even after knowing what you did to your previous partners."

After hearing this, she stared laughing.

Then the sage asked, "Now tell me who you really are?"

The prostitute replied to him and said, "I am this world."

"Did you understand the story, Jako?" he asked.

That was the best thing I ever heard in my entire life. I immediately knew what he was trying to say, I just had a flashback of my entire life in front of my eyes.

"See, there are things around us which are meant to be used, like our jobs, our assets, our vehicles etc. The tragedy is, we fall in love with them and we end up ruining everything. I think the cause of everything is our heedlessness. We think we know and understand everything but do we really know what we know? I remember you asked me about epistemology."

"Oh yeah, I remember when we first met," I said.

"That's right; it's something that keeps me away from heedlessness. And I am lucky that it's my career too. Just to remind you, I am talking about what we can choose and what we can't and what we should choose."

"Yes, I remember."

"Just add one more thing to the list of things we couldn't choose."

"Yeah, what?"

"Unfortunately we couldn't choose our teachers. We were forced to learn from people who called themselves teachers."

"But now we can choose and do whatever we want," I said.

"Sure we can, but we have spent a lot of time doing and studying something which helped us only to get a job. What about our inner self? What have we done to satisfy our curiosity?"

"Nothing, but whatever I studied has certainly enhanced my knowledge and intelligence. And I know something which I didn't know before," I said.

"Intelligence? Have you ever tried to figure out the meaning of being wise or wisdom?"

"Yeah, I know. Being wise is being smart and intelligent."

"But intelligence and wisdom have two different meanings in the dictionary. That means, wisdom is different from intelligence and indeed it is. An intelligent man may not be wise, whereas the wise person will be intelligent by default."

"I don't understand what you are trying to say."

"Let me tell you a story.

"Once there was a saint meditating in a cave all alone. A man came to him and interrupted his meditation and asked, 'What are you doing in this cave all alone?'

The saint replied to him, "I am meditating and trying to find God."

"Finding God?"

"Yes," the saint said.

Then the man said, "If you show me God and if I see him with my own eyes, I will believe in God."

The saint got up, held his hand and brought him out of the cave and said, "Look at the sun."

The man looked at the sun and said, "Are you joking? How can I see the sun? It's so bright. I can't stare at it."

Then the saint said, "How can you expect to see the creator, when you can't see the creation?"

"The moral is the wisdom of the saint. He was a wise man. If it had to be some intelligent person, he would have told him a few theories of existence and non-existence, and debated with him, using lengthy dialogues. That's the difference between wisdom and intellect. Wisdom is the short cut to reality. But it's sad to see that no one wants to know or study these things anymore. All we want is a good B school or a tech school in life. And when we realise that we were chasing the ghost all this time, we feel shaken up and run for solutions which we cannot pursue and we end up following cons like the one you came across in Goa. I think we should treat materials as materials and not fall for the so-called reality. The stupid thing that we do is not because we are dumb; it's because we don't see things clearly and we don't treat them the way they have to be treated."

"True man, I realise how foolish I was all this time. Wish I had seen things the way they are. I have kept blowing up things out of proportion all the time."

All of a sudden he asked, "You still miss your girl?"

"Trust me, not a single day goes by that I don't miss her. She has freaked me out."

"Did you love her?"

"I don't know whether it was infatuation or I loved her but yes, she is in my mind most of the time."

"But you show all the signs of infatuation. You can certainly live a beautiful life if you love someone. Even the pain that they give will be so sweet that you can't stop enjoying it. Do you think even she is restless like you are?"

"No certainly not. She might be enjoying her moments with another guy."

"You think she forgot you?"

"No, I don't think so."

"Then why do you worry, mate? You are the luckiest person."

"How is that?"

"You are restless because it was an infatuation and she is calm because she might have truly loved you. Because love makes people stay calm and content. There is a beautiful story to explain this proposition.

"There was a man who lived in a cave in ancient Persia for 70 years and he used to worship God every moment, out of love. And one day an angel descended to him. This angel was sent by God to deliver him a message."

The angel came inside the cave and spoke to that man, "God has sent me to deliver you a message."

The man got excited. He stood up and said, "I am so glad to hear that. What is the message that I have from my beloved?"

The angel replied, "All your prayers have been denied and your name is listed with the people who will go to hell. "

"After hearing this, the man started dancing and whirling out of joy as if he was waiting for that kind of a message."

The angel saw the man's state and said, "Are you stupid or insane?"

Then he replied, "You don't understand this state. This is what they call love. What do you think? I was worshipping him all my life to get my name in his good book? Or for some other reason? I worshipped him to get his attention. It doesn't matter where God puts me and I don't care if God writes my name in a good book or not. All I am ecstatic about is that, God took my name and thought about me. Isn't that what all the lovers demand?"

After listening to the story, there was some kind of peace that was settling over my heart. This was the first time I had this kind of a feeling.

"Now tell me Mr. Jackson, what do you really want?"

"I want loads of money, man, loads of them."

"Why?"

"Because I can go wherever I want to go."

"Why?"

"So that I can do whatever I want to do."

"Why do you want to do whatever you want to do?"

"Because I want to be happy."

"That's what I thought you would say. It all comes and culminates into happiness, isn't it?"

"Yes, that's the goal of everything. But I think happiness is just a state of mind and our mood keeps changing every now and then, so we can't be happy and sad for too long."

"Okay, now tell me. If there is a spark, we can assume there is a fire, right?"

"Yes."

"On that note we can also assume, when there is happiness for a limited time, there is a possibility that it can stay for longer than we could imagine?"

"Probably yes, but how can we be happy all the time?"

"That's the real problem. The moment you try to secure happiness, that's exactly when you lose it. Can you tell me at least one thing that you tried to secure in your life and succeeded? I don't think so. And yes we need a medium to reach happiness; the point is which medium are you going to choose? And I forgot to mention one thing when I was talking about wise people. The wise ones are always happy because happiness is a selfish thing and they acknowledge it appropriately.

"But, we on the other end, never acknowledge our selfishness. Just look at us, you are sitting here with me because you are selfish. You may have needed a break and I may be giving that to you, please don't take me wrong. Even I am selfish here. I may be sitting here because I wanted to kill time and I needed a company for camping, so I chose you. Even our friends for that matter, they need us because they want to have fun and our parents raise us because they have their own expectation. Even your girlfriend was with you for her own selfish needs. All I am trying to say is that constant happiness can be achieved only when we consider ourselves to be selfish and if we proceed in the right direction."

"Right direction uh? But who decides what is right and what is wrong?" I asked.

He looked at me and gave a wide smile.

"What happened?" I asked.

"Certainly not religion, if you are looking that as an answer. It's actually us who decide what is right and wrong; good or bad, through our own perceptions because we always get impressed by our own perceptions. The reason is, perceptions are usually formed from our past experiences. There is the story of an oilman and his parrot:

"Once, an oilman possessed a talking parrot, which used to amuse him all the time. One day he left his shop for some work and asked the parrot to look after the shop. A cat came inside the shop and dropped a few bottles and broke them. The oil got spilled all over the floor. When the oilman returned, he thought that the parrot had done this mischief, and in his anger he smacked the parrot so hard that all its feathers dropped off and the parrot couldn't speak for few days after that."

One day a bald-headed man walked into the shop. The parrot had recovered its speech by then and said, "Hey, whose oil did you spill?"

"Although the story is funny, we are exactly like that parrot. We trust our instincts more than we should. To us, our opinions are superior to anything that exists. When we can't stop praising our self, how can we praise something else?"

"But who are we to decide? Isn't it Nature's law? Few things are meant to be good and right and others are bad and wrong," I said.

"This is the basic human error I think. There is nothing evil or bad from the beginning. How can anything be wrong or evil from the beginning? How can you create anything bad when there is no good before that? Let me put it this way; there is nothing called Bad. It's the absence of good which turns something bad. Similarly; nothing is dangerous, lack of safety makes it dangerous. In the same way, there is nothing called a lie; it's just the absence of the truth. Even if you see it scientifically, lack of heat turns something cold. And if you go even further, there is nothing called darkness; it's just the absence of light. Have you ever seen a torch which flashes darkness? The idea is, there is nothing as bad, evil, wrong from its very beginning. There has to be something perfect and when it loses its perfection, then it becomes imperfect."

"Ah, I know how it works now. And then I saw birds flying, they were not owls or bats. What's the time?" I asked.

"Its 4:30 a.m.," he said.

"Oh my God, now I am convinced with the theory of relativity. I didn't realise how the time flew. Did we spend the whole night talking?"

"Oh yes, that's what it looks like," he said.

I think building the tent didn't do any good to us, except that we kept our belonging in that. I was tired and sleepy by then, and sleeping there was a bad idea. I asked Hami if we could go back to the shack to sleep; and he agreed. I helped him take off the tent, and we left the place around 5 a.m. in the morning. We reached the shack in about one and half hours.

"What's the plan for tomorrow?" he asked.

"Anything you say boss, I have all the time," I said.

"So when are you planning to get up?"

"Maybe by afternoon," I said.

"Okay, knock at my door if you get up early."

"You don't have any plans to sleep?" I asked.

"Not exactly, I am going to the town. Need to check my e-mails. "

"Sure, I'll catch you later."

Ah, what a wonderful night I had. I felt elevated and content. I was not the same person that I was earlier. I came and slept without any constraints, hoping to talk to Hami in the evening. I slept without any fear and troubles, and I woke up around 3 p.m. I went to Hami's shack and found it locked. He was at the restaurant sitting at his usual table, reading the newspaper. As I walked towards him, he looked at me and said, "Good morning, troubled soul."

"Thanks for calling me by my real name," I laughed. "You didn't sleep?" I asked.

"No buddy, I had to do the packing."

"Packing? What for?"

"Oh, I have to leave tonight. I booked my tickets."

"All of a sudden?"

"There are some issues with my visa. I am going to Mumbai and I'll take off from there."

I didn't know what to say at that moment. I felt like asking him not to leave. But how could I do that? Though he was a stranger, he mattered most to me now.

"You can't do your work over phone from here?" I asked.

"I wish I could, but I need to be there."

I wished I could I kidnap and hide him somewhere and ask him everything that I was curious about. But again, it'll be like the story of a foolish man who killed the goose which used to lay the golden eggs. May be I should just let him go. Like he said, we should sacrifice something to keep it with us forever.

"So what time is your bus?" I asked.

"At 8 p.m."

"So you are getting back to your life, uh?"

"Not sure about that, mate. How about you? How long are you planning to stay?"

"I don't know. I am afraid to get back to my usual life."

15
The Culmination

He asked me to take a seat, and said, "Pardon me, mate but I have figured out your problems. How long are you planning to run from your problems? I know that life is full of exits, but it doesn't mean that we have to take an exit every time we face a difficulty. We are born to face difficulties, man. Don't you know what pain we go through when we come to this world? It's not the survival of the fittest; it's the survival of the wisest. And there is no escape from difficulties and whosoever claims to provide a permanent solution from the difficulties is a fool himself and he or she will lead you astray.

"There is always a solution to all our problems. They say water existed before the thirst; we have problems because there is a solution to them. And to be honest, things get a lot worse before they get better. If you lose yourself, consider that you have lost everything. And right now, you don't look like you've lost yourself. There is still time to see things clearly. All you need to do is stand for yourself and say, these things are not real and it doesn't make any sense to me, exactly like the story of the emperor who had no clothes. What matters is the pleasure at the end of the day and you have to understand when there is a temporary pleasure, it's a clue that there is everlasting pleasure too.

"Like I said earlier, wisdom is the key to the mysteries of life and this world, and it can be achieved when you know the reality of every aspect of things that's around you. Everybody is wise from their birth and their heedlessness makes them stupid. You are *Wisely Stupid* right now. Try shedding your heedlessness first because that opens the door for you. In heedlessness, we try to derive pleasure even when we are losing ourselves.

"Want to listen to an eye-opening story?"

"Perhaps, the last one."

"A man was running for his life, being chased by a furious lion in a jungle. While he was running, he suddenly noticed a well and without a second thought, he immediately jumped into it to save his life. Before he could land inside, he saw a python inside the well and it looked like it was waiting for him. He then held a rope which was hanging. The man felt safe holding the rope and he thought it saved him. But the lion was looking into the well from the top. Shortly after he held the rope, two mice (one was white and another one was black) crawled up on the rope and started nibbling on it. The rope weakened in a moment, while the python and lion were waiting for him desperately. In between all this, he saw a honeycomb and he couldn't resist. He stuck his finger into it and started tasting the honey in spite of all the dangers that surrounded him.

"Now, reflect on the story by keeping these things in your mind. The lion was his death which chases a man constantly. The python was his grave which was waiting for him. The rope was his life which he tried to hold on to and finally the black and white mice were his days and nights which were nibbling at the duration of his life. With all these troubles around, due to his heedlessness the man still wanted to enjoy and that's why he started licking the honey.

"With all due respect, my friend, it seems like life, which is your horse, is riding you instead of you riding it. You have to conquer the things in you, which are out of your control and break the invisible cage which you live in. How long are you planning to follow others? You have a mind of your own and you have suppressed it throughout your life by getting influenced by the so-called real things.

"There are thousand types of knowledge in this world, mate. Acquire only those which benefit you because time has a limit. Death is not the end because it was not the beginning. Say good morning to yourself no matter at what time you wake up. Our instinct of following others will never stop. Even animals have this tendency. Haven't you seen ducklings follow the ducks and learn how to swim just by imitating? The question is, who do you want to follow? I think by now you have an idea about what to expect and what not to. Imagine yourself as a gardener whose job is only to water the plants; your job is not to worry about the fruits because it's not in your hand. All you can do is to water it regularly.

"If you need answers for everything and if you want to satisfy your curiosity, start knowing yourself. When you don't know yourself, how can you know something which is out of yourself?"

After saying this, he took out a yellow coloured card from his journal and gave it to me. There was something written in black ink in amazing calligraphy. He gave to me and said, "It's for you."

I think it was a gift for me. It was a poem and it explained everything…

Your cure is within you, but you do not know,
Your illness is from you, but you do not see.
You are the 'Clarifying Book'
Through whose letters manifest the hidden.
You suppose that you're a small body,
But the greatest world unfolds within you.
You would not need what is outside of yourself,
If you would reflect upon self, but you do not reflect.

"This is best thing that I ever read. Did you write this?"

"No, it's not mine. Did you like it?"

"Oh, it's wonderful."

"There are thousands like these. If you like this or something similar to this, you'll be drawn towards it. Do not worry."

"But where can I find all these? How will I find all the answers to my questions?" I asked.

He smiled and said, "If things were easy to find, they are not worth finding. Like I said earlier, your answers are within you. You have to figure it out yourself by using all the tools you've got. As I see, you are using only one tool from your tool-box. And keep logic and reasoning as your base when you search for things and be steadfast in whatever you do, no matter what, because you are the best architect of yourself."

"I don't knew what destiny has stored for me, Hami."

"See, again you are triggering a problem. Destiny is something which cannot be talked about. We have to live to find it out. Age is the high price to pay for the maturity my friend and don't end up paying that."

"I understand, but I have gone through so much that I can barely hold myself. I feel like I can never break the cage that I live in."

"I know you are in grief, Jako, but don't turn your grief into anger. If you do that, it'll never leave you. And maybe there is a reason that you are in this cage; only sweet singing birds get caught. Have you ever seen a crow or an owl being caged? There is a saying, 'If you are getting irritated by every rub, how will you be polished?' All you have to do is to check you potential and see how far you can exceed your abilities in this isolation. If you collapse now, you'll be injured and this injury can spoil your war in the future."

After consoling me, Hami gave me his visiting card and said, "you happen to visit UK, just drop by." And then he went inside and brought his luggage out. It was time for him to leave. I volunteered to drop him to the bus stand. The bus was on time and I helped him board the bus. I shook his hand for the last time and said, "You were awesome. Thank you for whatever you shared with me."

He looked into my eyes, smiled and said, "This is a kind of praise which I don't deserve and it's a kind of insult that you don't deserve."

I stood there till the bus left and I walked 10 kms back to the shack. All the way, I couldn't think of anything, all my senses were numb. When I reached the shack, Chandu looked at me and said, "Sir, did your friend leave?" I didn't reply to him verbally, I nodded and walked inside my shack. I started packing my luggage as there was no point staying here anymore. I finished my dinner and told Chandu about my plans. Later on in the dark night, I walked to the beach and sat at our usual spot all alone. I was back to where I had started from. But this time I was rehabilitated. It's time for me to do the real introspection for the first time.

No doubt, Hami was like a rain in drought, he helped me see myself. Calling him a guardian angel will be dramatic, but he helped me without any expectations. Now I could do quality thinking before I formed a thought. I have no shame in acknowledging that half of my troubles are self-invited. I was chasing ghosts all this while and now I know what matters and what doesn't. I thought I could run away from everything and indeed I was running all this while, but when I look back, I am still here. It's like I was running on an invisible treadmill.

I am glad that I was tested by so many trials and tribulations. Now I can expose my true quality. I had reached the point of committing suicide because I considered my girlfriend, my family, job, friends, education and my niche as everything. It was because I was emotionally challenged due to my own ignorance. But when I saw someone lying all alone in a grave, it was then that I realised the reality of life. Wow! What an amazing event that was, which helped me flee away from my so-called life. I think I would have tried to commit suicide again after a few days if I hadn't visited that graveyard.

Indeed, this world is full of suffering, but there are elements to cure it. Now I am convinced that if something has to come to me, it will come to me no matter what happens and no one can stop that. And if something is not meant for me, I will not get it no matter how much I try to get it. I was just travelling with my worries and troubles, and I met Hami without any effort. Isn't that enough? I never asked him to substantiate on whatever he told me. I think sometimes we have to agree and accept wise things without asking for a proof to check whether it's logical and reasonable.

If I plan something from now, again it will be the cause of tragedy. The truth is, we can't change the past, we can only hope for a better future. Seriously! Don't I know the logic now? Although I plan, someone else would also plan and he is the best of planners. I should let my destiny unfold its mysteries, instead of meddling with it. The best I can do in my future is, not to accompany someone whose being does not inspire me.

I will leave this place tomorrow morning. I am ready to treat things the way they deserve to be treated. I will quit the job and create something on my own, or I will go and meet Hami and study more, because it's nothing like owning yourself. I should bring out what's inside me, instead of doing or creating something with things which are already present out there.

I have no animosity or grudge towards anything whatsoever. And given a chance, I would like to meet Deepa for the last time because I didn't like the way our last conversation ended. Not only her, given a chance, I would like to fix and tie all the loose ends of my life. I have thrown the diamonds in the lake, mistaking them for stones in the darkness. Now I know what diamonds are; I can recognise them even in darkness.

'Promised land' is where I hold on to the promises that I have made to myself. I was wrong that there are no answers. There are answers; it's just that I was knocking the wrong doors. May be, I was striving for something which was already granted to me.

I thought I was done when I was buying those ropes to tie a hanging knot. But now, I have shown myself the paths which no one can comprehend. There is no such thing as perfect destiny; sometimes the road becomes your destiny.

If there is a God out there, I have an idea about how it works. If I can't see him, maybe because he's extremely close to me, in the same way as I can't see the retina of my eyes. If he alienates me from others, maybe he wants to open the door of intimacy with him and when he gives me something, he is showing me his kindness. And if he deprives me, he is showing me his power. And in all that, he is making himself known to me and showering me with all his gentleness.

❍❍❍

Kindly share your reviews about this book with other readers on Amazon.in

TOP 10 BOOKS OF GENERAL PRESS

- » Relativity by Albert Einstein
  Science/Physics, ISBN : 9789380914220

- » Student's Encyclopedia of General Knowledge
  Children's Non-Fiction/GK, ISBN : 9789380914190

- » The Diary of a Young Girl by Anne Frank
  Autobiography/Memoir, ISBN : 9789380914312

- » Siddhartha by Hermann Hesse
  Literature & Fiction/Classic, ISBN : 9789380914145

- » Know Your Worth by Sondhi & Vibha
  Slef-Help/Success, ISBN : 9788180320231

- » The Gita Way by Shweta and Santosh
  Religion/Hindu, ISBN : 9789380914879

- » Love Happens only Once by Rochak Bhatnagar
  Literature & Fiction/Romance, ISBN : 9789380914183

- » One Life, One Love by Rochak Bhatnagar
  Literature & Fiction/Romance, ISBN : 9789380914350

- » The Girl I Last Loved by Smita Kaushik
  Literature & Fiction/Romance, ISBN : 9789380914244

- » Because...Every Raindrop is a Hope by Sankalp Kohli
  Literature & Fiction/Romance, ISBN : 9789380914435

Develop your reading habit | Gift books to your friends

www.ingramcontent.com/pod-product-compliance
Ingram Content Group UK Ltd.
Pitfield, Milton Keynes, MK11 3LW, UK
UKHW042003190726
13854UKWH00005B/2139

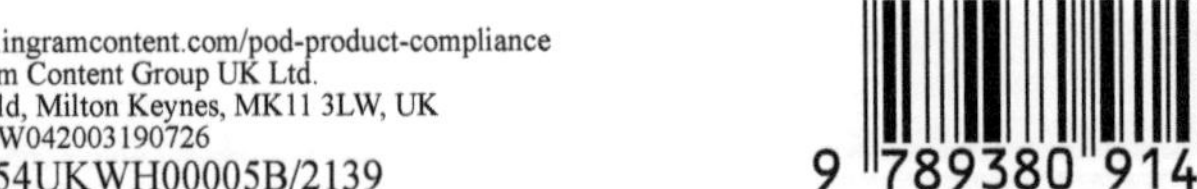

9 789380 914398